"Do you have any other weapons?"

"If I did, I'd have used them already," Esme said.

"Mind if I check? Just to be sure?"

"Yes. I do."

"I'm going to have to do it anyway. You could make it easier by not struggling."

"You could make it easier by letting me go."

"That would defeat the purpose of me and King spending the last three days hanging around Long Pine Key Campground searching for you."

"Is that Cujo's name? King?"

"Yeah. Why?" Ian patted her down one-handed, refusing to release his hold. No matter how small she seemed, no matter how harmless, she was part of the crime family that had killed his parents.

* * *

CLASSIFIED K-9 UNIT:
These lawmen solve the toughest cases
with the help of their brave canine partners

Aside from her faith and her family, there's not much **Shirlee McCoy** enjoys more than a good book! When she's not teaching or chauffeuring her five kids, she can usually be found plotting her next Love Inspired Suspense story or wandering around the beautiful Inland Northwest in search of inspiration. Shirlee loves to hear from readers. If you have time, drop her a line at shirlee@shirleemccoy.com.

BODYGUARD

SHIRLEE McCOY

HARLEQUIN® LOVE INSPIRED® SUSPENSE

Special thanks and acknowledgment to Shirlee McCoy for her participation in the Classified K-9 Unit miniseries.

Recycling programs for this product may not exist in your area.

LOVE INSPIRED BOOKS

ISBN-13: 978-0-373-45722-9

Bodyguard

www.Harlequin.com

Printed in U.S.A.

Have I not commanded you? Be strong and courageous.
Do not be afraid, do not be discouraged. For the
Lord your God will be with you wherever you go.
—Joshua 1:9

To my beautiful and brave niece, Aaliyah Parker.
The strongest young lady I know. I am so proud of you
and so blessed to call you family! Keep smiling, sweetie.
And, I will keep praying! I love you dearly!

ONE

If the Everglades didn't kill her, her uncle would.

Either way, Esme Dupree was going to die.

The thought of that—of all the things she'd leave behind, all the dreams she'd never fulfill—had kept her moving through the Florida wetland for three days, but she was tiring. Even the most determined person in the world couldn't keep running forever. And she'd been running for what seemed like nearly that long. First, she'd fled witness protection, crisscrossing states to try to stay a step ahead of her uncle's henchmen. She'd finally found her way to Florida, to the thick vegetation and quiet waterways that her parents had loved.

Esme wasn't as keen. Her family had spent every summer of her childhood here, exploring the wetland, documenting flora and fauna as part of Esme's home-school experience. She preferred open fields and prairie grass, but her parents had loved the shallow green water of the Everglades. She'd never had the heart to tell them that she didn't. By that time, her older siblings were grown and gone, and it was just the three of them, exploring the world together.

Funny that she'd come back here when her life was

falling apart; when everything she'd worked for had been shot to smithereens by her brother's and uncle's crimes, Esme had returned to a place filled with fond memories.

It was also filled with lots of things that could kill a person. Alligators. Crocodiles. Snakes. Panthers. She wasn't as worried about those as she was about human predators.

Her uncle and the people he'd hired.

The FBI, too. If they tracked her down, they wouldn't kill her, but she'd put her hope in them before, trusted them for her safety. She'd almost died because of it.

She wiped sweat from her brow and sipped water from her canteen. Better to go it alone than to count on people who couldn't be depended on. She'd been learning that the hard way these past few months.

Bugs dive-bombed every inch of her exposed flesh, the insect repellant sweating off almost as quickly as she could spray it on. Things hadn't been so bad when she'd been renting a little trailer at the edge of the national park. She'd had shelter from the bugs and the critters. But Uncle Angus had tracked her down and nearly killed her. He would have killed her if she hadn't smashed his head with a snow globe and called the police. They'd come quickly.

Of course they had.

They were as eager to get their hands on her as Uncle Angus had been. It seemed like every law enforcement office in the United States was keeping its eyes out for her.

Thanks to the feds, the organization that had sworn to protect her. Witness protection was supposed to be her ticket out of the mess she'd found herself in. She'd hoped it would be. She'd probably even believed it would. She'd entered the program because she'd seen her brother murder a man in cold blood. She'd seen the look in his eyes, and she'd known that he was capable of anything. Even killing her to keep her quiet. What she'd learned since then was that there was no panacea to her trouble. No easy way out. No certain solution. Her best hope was in herself and her ability to keep a step ahead of her uncle until the trial.

"That might have been easier if you'd stayed with the police," she muttered, using a long wooden pole to move the canoe through shallow water.

There was no sense beating herself up over the decision to run again. Uncle Angus's hired guns had fire-bombed the tiny police station she'd been taken to after she'd been attacked. During the chaos that had followed, she'd seen the opportunity and she'd run.

It had seemed like the right decision at the time.

Now she wasn't so sure. The sun had nearly set, its golden glow still lingering on the horizon. Mosquitoes buzzed around her head. She didn't bother slapping at them. Her arms ached. Her head throbbed. Her body felt leaden. All she wanted was to get out of the Glades and back to civilization. She'd make different decisions this time. Head for a place she'd never been before. She'd buy colored contacts to change the bright green eyes she'd inherited from her mother. The reading glasses she'd bought and worn hadn't hidden them well enough, and Uncle Angus had told her that was how she'd been found.

"Those eyes, kid," he'd growled. "You can't hide them."

He was wrong. She could, and she would.

No more living in her delusions, telling herself that everything was going to be okay because she was a good person with a good heart who wanted only what was best for the people she loved.

A fool.

Because she really wanted to believe that good begat good and that the happily-ever-after she'd planned for so many clients would happen for her one day.

She might be a fool, but she wasn't stupid.

If she was found again, she *would* die.

But she wasn't going to be found. She'd sleep in the canoe again. Just like she had the past three nights, covered by mosquito netting, listening to things slither in and out of the water. By tomorrow afternoon, she should reach her destination—Long Pine Key Campground. She eyed the compass she'd bought before she'd left Wyoming, using a small Mag light to study the map she'd grabbed from the Everglades National Park information center.

She'd had a feeling she was going to need both.

As a matter of fact, she'd put together a survival pack, and she'd hidden it in the crumbling loft of one of the boat sheds that dotted the trailer park where she'd been staying.

She'd been able to grab it after she'd escaped the police.

Maybe she wasn't as much of a fool as her ex-fiancé, Brent, had said she was when she'd told him she was going to testify against her brother. She *was* tired, though. Tired people made mistakes. Like coming to the Everglades instead of heading for Texas or California or somewhere else where no one would think to look for her.

Death.

It had been stalking her for months, but now...

Now she could feel it breathing down her neck.

She shuddered, watching the edges of the murky water for a place to pull onto the shore. She needed a spot clear of vegetation. One that would allow her to drag the canoe far away from the edge of the water.

Tomorrow she'd be away from the slithering, slapping, plopping sounds of things moving through the water. She'd leave the canoe behind and make her way out of Florida. She still had money. Not much, but enough to get her to another state. She'd start fresh, build a new business. Nothing to do with weddings or brides. Nothing that anyone she knew would connect her with.

Not even Violetta.

Her eyes burned at the thought of never seeing her older sister again, her heart heavy with what that would mean—no family, no connections, no one who shared all her childhood memories.

If she could have, she'd have contacted her sister. But she didn't dare. Their brother, Reginald, would use Violetta's knowledge about Esme to his advantage. He'd probably been doing it all along. As much as she loved her sister, she also knew Violetta's weakness—greed. She liked the good things in life, and she was happy to let their brother, Reginald, give them to her. Even if his means to those ends was murder.

Esme winced at the thought, pushing aside the memory that was always at the back of her mind. She'd witnessed a murder. Her brother had been the murderer. She'd watched the victim die, and she'd known that she couldn't keep quiet.

She'd turned on her family, betraying the deepest of all bonds.

That was what Uncle Angus had said when he'd broken into the trailer.

Turned on family, and that makes you the lowest of low. You have to die, Esme. Because family is everything.

It *was* a lot, but there was more to life. There was integrity, there was honor, there was faith. The last was what had enabled her to offer herself as a witness to her brother's crimes. She had what no one else in her family did—a certainty that God was in control, that He'd work everything out for His good.

She just hoped His good didn't involve her dying in the middle of the Florida wetland.

Esme flashed her light along the edges of the water, ready to stop for the night, to try to shut off her thoughts and get some sleep. Somewhere in the distance, a dog barked, the sound both alarming and comforting. She had to be on the right track, moving closer to civilization. The map and the compass hadn't steered her wrong, but civilization meant people, and that meant more danger.

Her light shone on marshy land. Eyes peered out from thick foliage, and she tried not to let herself think about what was watching her. She didn't mind the mammals. Mice, marsh rats, deer. Even thinking about panthers and bears didn't bother her. It was the reptiles that made her skin crawl—alligators, crocodiles, snakes.

"Cut it out!" she whispered, her voice filled with the fear she'd been working hard not to acknowledge. Oh, what she wouldn't give to be back in her cute little Chicago apartment, making dinner after a long day planning weddings.

Esme sighed. She did not want to be in a place where predators were waiting to do what they did best.

The dog barked again—a quick sharp sound that made her wonder if she were even closer to civilization than she'd originally thought. She'd already planned her escape route and knew—in theory—how to get from the dock at the trailer park to the closest Everglade car-accessible campground. If cars could get in, she could walk out. And that was what she planned to do.

Her light glanced off what looked like a tiny boathouse, the old wood structure gray against the lush vegetation. She checked her map, circling the camping area she thought she'd arrived at. The glades were dotted with little places like this—areas where a couple of campers could bed down for the night. This time of year, though, the water was high and the risk was greater. There weren't as many campers. Just die-hard naturalists and explorers who wanted adventure.

Esme was neither of those things.

She liked home and books and routine.

She hated scary movies, danger, intrigue.

All she'd wanted was to plan weddings, marry her college sweetheart, have the nice life she'd been dreaming of for years.

But here she was.

Ready to bed down for another night in a place that she'd rather not be.

She steered toward the wood structure, saw the clearing beyond it. There were lights in the distance—unexpected signs that she really was closer to civilization than she thought.

Esme dragged the canoe out of the water, her waders sucked in by the muddy ground. Behind her, something splashed, and she imagined a crocodile or giant snapping turtle moving toward her.

There were no other boats, no campers, nothing human that she could see. Whatever the light had been, it was gone now. Twilight turned the world deep purple, casting long shadows across the wet ground.

She climbed into the boat, traced the route she'd highlighted on the map, double- and triple-checking her coordinates. Two more camping spots before she reached her destination. Unless she'd missed a couple on the journey.

That was a possibility.

If she had, she might be at the last stop before the road-accessible campground. Something rustled in the brush, and she jumped, scanning the area, looking for whatever had made the noise. Not a mouse or rat. This had sounded large. A panther? A bear? Her heart thudded in her chest as she pulled the bowie knife from the sheath she'd strapped to her thigh. It glinted in the last rays of the setting sun, the blade new and wicked-looking. A great weapon for fighting something close-up, but she'd prefer to keep far from whatever was lurking in the shadows. In hindsight, a gun would have been a better idea. Purchasing a firearm would have been a problem, but she could have gotten her hands on one if she'd tried hard enough.

It wasn't like she didn't know how to use one. Her parents had taught her, and Reginald had reiterated the importance of knowing how to defend herself. Probably because he'd been afraid that his crimes would catch up to him, that the people he'd hurt would come back to hurt his family.

Family was everything, but he hadn't loved his enough to keep them out of harm's way. The irony of that wasn't lost on her.

The bushes rustled again—closer this time. Whatever it was, it was stalking her. She could feel it coming closer, see leaves shifting and plants shivering as something moved past.

"Please, God," she whispered, her fingers so tight around the knife hilt they ached. "Please."

And then it was on her, springing out from the brush in a flash of dark fur and dark eyes, her light following the movement as she scrambled back. Her knife hand moving as her brain screamed the truth—

A dog!

The *thing* was a dog, bounding across the open ground and stopping beside her. Sniffing at the air, at the boat, its nose so close she could have touched it.

"Hello," she said, her voice shaking, but the dog was already bounding away, barking wildly, the bright orange vest it was wearing glowing in the beam of Esme's light.

It took a second for that to register.

The vest.

The dog.

A search team. Either her uncle's henchmen or the police.

Looking for her.

She jumped out of the canoe, dragged it back toward the water, her heart slamming against her ribs as she tried desperately to escape whoever was on her trail.

The lady was back in the water, tugging the canoe out of the shallows. She probably thought she could escape again, but Esme Dupree was about to be disappointed.

Ian Slade sprinted the last few yards that separated him from his quarry, his K-9 partner, King, barking ferociously beside him. Esme had to know they were coming, but she didn't glance back, didn't stop, she just kept dragging the canoe, splashing through the green water, alerting every predator in the area that prey was moving through.

He grabbed her arm, was surprised when she swung around, a bowie knife clutched in her free hand.

King growled low in his throat, a warning that Esme would be wise to heed. The Belgian Malinois was trained in protection. Smart, agile and strong, King had a bite as vicious as his bark.

"My partner," Ian warned, "doesn't like when people threaten me."

"Is that what I'm doing?" She tried to pull away, but after three days of tracking her, there was no way Ian planned to let her go.

"What would you call it?" he replied, dragging her back a few steps.

"Defending myself."

King growled again, and Esme's gaze shifted, her attention caught just long enough for Ian to make his move.

He disarmed her with ease, grabbing her knife arm and twisting it until she dropped the weapon. Even then, he didn't release his hold.

Sure, her record was clean. She made a living planning weddings…pretty aboveboard, from the looks of it. But Esme was a member of the Dupree crime family, cut from the same cloth as her brother—a man who killed first and asked questions later.

Ian knew that more than most.

She yanked against his hold, forcing her arm into an angle that had to be painful. He might not trust her, but he didn't want to hurt her.

"Calm down," he said, shifting his grip. "I'm Agent Ian Slade. With the FBI.'"

"And that's supposed to be comforting?" Esme ground out as she continued to tug against his hold.

"More comforting than staying out in the middle of nowhere with your uncle still on the loose."

"He wouldn't be loose if your team would focus on apprehending him rather than me." She yanked hard, her boots slipping in the muck.

She'd have gone down if he weren't holding on to her.

She didn't seem to realize that there was no way she was going to escape. Ian was a well-trained federal officer, part of an elite group of agents. He was also a head taller than she was and seventy pounds heavier. Maybe more. Her bones were small, her wrist tiny, his hand circling it with ease.

As battles went, this wasn't a fair one, and he almost felt bad for restraining her.

Almost.

He knew what her family was capable of.

Until she proved differently, he had to assume she was capable of the same. Even if he'd been one-hundred-percent certain that she wasn't, he wouldn't have let her go. Protecting her was his assignment. Keeping her alive until the case against her brother went to trial was what he'd agreed to do.

Despite the fact that she was a Dupree.

"Do you have any other weapons on you?" he asked, his fingers curved around her wrist. She'd stopped tugging. Maybe she'd finally realized she couldn't get away.

"If I did, I'd have used them already," she spat.

"On a federal officer?" he asked.

"I didn't realize you were a federal officer at first. If I had, I wouldn't have pulled the knife."

"Good to know. Mind if I make sure you're telling the truth about weapons?"

"Yes. I do."

He could have forced the issue, but there wasn't any point. She might try to run, but he didn't think she'd attack him to do it. She had a clean record, no history of violence or trouble.

"All right," he said, releasing her.

"Thanks." She started walking to the canoe as if she thought he'd let her leave.

"I'm not checking for a weapon, but I'm not letting you leave, either."

"It would be easier on both of us if you did." She turned to face him, the darkening evening wrapping her in shadows. He couldn't see her expression through the gloom, but he could see the pale oval of her face, the tension in her shoulders.

"That would defeat the purpose of me and King spending the last three days hanging around Long Pine Key Campground waiting for you to show up."

"I didn't ask you to come looking for me. As a matter of fact, I would have preferred that you didn't, Agent Slade," she responded.

"Ian. We'll be spending a lot of time together. We might as well be on a first-name basis."

"I'm not going back into witness protection."

"That's fine. We'll work something else out."

"I guess I should have been more clear. I'm not going back into any kind of federal protection. I've been on my own for a few months now, and I've been doing just fine."

"Until your uncle tracked you down," he pointed out, and she stiffened.

"I was tracked down long before I came to Florida," she responded. "Or have you forgotten that poor woman who was murdered because she was in the same state you'd hidden me in?"

He hadn't forgotten.

None of the members of the team had.

Information about Esme's location had been leaked to the Dupree crime family, and a woman who'd looked a lot like her had been killed. "I'm sorry that happened. More than I can express, but I'm not part of the witness protection unit. I work for the FBI Tactical K-9 Unit."

"It doesn't matter who you work for. I'm not spending any more time with you."

"I wish that was how things worked, but it isn't. You agreed to testify against your brother."

"And I plan to."

"That will be really difficult to do if you're dead."

"If I'd stayed in Wyoming, I probably would be. Then we wouldn't be having this conversation."

She had a point. A good one. Esme was the sole witness to a murder her brother had committed. Her brother, Reginald, and Angus would do anything to keep her from testifying.

"We had a security breach," he explained, snagging her backpack from the bottom of the canoe. "It won't happen again."

"It won't happen again because I'm not going back into protective custody."

"I'm afraid you are."

She narrowed her eyes at him. "Have you ever been wrong before?"

"More than I'd like to be."

"Good," she retorted. "Then you won't be upset that

you're wrong this time." She whirled around and would have walked away, but King blocked her path, pressing in close to her legs.

She shot a look in Ian's direction, her eyes still flashing with anger. "Call off your dog."

"Release," he said, and King pranced back to his side.

"Thanks." She probably would have walked away, but he held up her pack.

"Forgetting something?"

She reached for it and King growled.

"He doesn't like people taking things from me."

"I don't like people touching my things," she responded, her focus on King. She looked scared. He didn't blame her. At home, King was goofy and friendly, funny and entertaining. On the job, he was intimidating, his tan face and dark muzzle giving him a wolf-like appearance.

"Sorry. I've got to check the contents before we move out."

"I think I made it clear that—"

"You plan on going it alone. You've made it very clear. Unfortunately, my job is to get you to trial safely. I can't do that if we're not together."

"We're at cross purposes, then, and I don't see us finding common ground." She stepped back, and he thought she might be looking for an escape route. One that King wouldn't be able to follow.

"The common ground is this—we both want to keep you alive. How about you let me do what I'm trained to do?"

"Which is?"

"Protecting people like you."

King growled, the sound low and mean.

Esme froze, but Ian could have told her the growl wasn't directed at her. It was a warning. One that sent adrenaline shooting through Ian's bloodstream. He grabbed Esme's wrist, dragging her close.

"What—" she began, but Ian held up his hand, silencing her so that he could listen. The evening had gone eerily quiet, King's rumbling growl the only sound.

He pulled Esme to the thick brush that surrounded the campsite, motioning for her to drop down into the cover it offered. She slipped into the summer-soft leaves silently, folding herself down so that even he could barely see her.

King swiveled, tracking something that Ian could neither see nor hear. He wanted to think that it was a panther, a bear, an alligator, but King was trained to differentiate between human and animal threats. Besides, thanks to former team member Jake Morrow, the Dupree crime family seemed to always be just one step behind the K-9 team. There was every possibility that one or more of Angus's henchmen was wandering through the Everglades.

He thrust Esme's backpack into her arms, leaning close to whisper in her ear. "Stay down. Stay quiet. Don't move."

She nodded, clutching the backpack to her chest.

King's growl changed pitch. Whoever was coming was getting closer. It wasn't local law enforcement, and it wasn't a member of the K-9 team. They were back at headquarters waiting for word that Ian had finally found Esme's trail.

That left only one other option.

Angus Dupree or his hired guns.

Ian acted quickly, shoving the canoe into the water

with just enough force to keep it moving. He gave King the signal to heel and went with him into the shelter of thick vegetation. Mosquitoes and flies buzzed around King's head, but the dog didn't move; his attention was fixed on a spot just beyond the clearing. Ian knew the area. He'd walked it several times the past few days, certain that Esme would arrive there eventually.

She was smart.

There was no doubt about that.

Ian had done his research. He knew as much as there was to know about her childhood, her schooling, her college years. He knew she'd built her business without the help of her older sister, that she'd never taken a dime from her brother. Everything she had, she'd earned on the right side of the law by using the brain God had given her.

The fact that she'd escaped witness protection and had stayed under the radar for months was even more proof of her keen intelligence. Smart people didn't go into situations without a plan. Ian had visited the trailer she'd been renting at the edge of the Everglades. He'd seen the old boathouse and the dock, and he'd known she'd had an escape route in mind when she'd chosen to rent the place.

All he'd needed was a map and a highlighter. He'd done some calculations, tried to think of how far someone like Esme would be willing to travel in a hostile environment. It hadn't taken any time at all to figure out that the quickest, most direct route out of the Everglades brought her here.

He'd staked out the area, walking a grid pattern every day, waiting for her to show.

Apparently, he wasn't the only one who'd been haunting this place looking for her. She was smart, but she'd have been better off leaving the area. She hadn't had the backpack with her while she was in protective custody with the local police, and she hadn't visited any of the local outdoor supply stores, either. He had to assume that she'd returned to the rental to retrieve the pack. Which meant there was something she needed in it. Money seemed more likely than anything.

King's growl had become a deep rumble of unease. Scruff standing on end, muscles taut, he waited for the signal to go in. Ian waited, too. He didn't know how many people were approaching or what kind of fire-power they'd brought. Backup was already on the way. He'd called in to headquarters as soon as he'd seen Esme paddling toward the campsite.

A shadow appeared a hundred yards out, and King crouched, ready to bound toward it. Ian gave him the signal to hold, watching as two more people stepped into view. A posse of three hunting a lone woman. If Esme had been bedded down for the night, they'd have been on her before she'd realized what was happening.

An unfair fight, but that was the way the Duprees did things.

One of the men turned on a flashlight, the beam bouncing across the camping area and flashing on the water. Twenty feet from the shore, the canoe floated languidly.

"There!" the man hollered, pulling a gun, the world exploding in a hail of gunfire.

TWO

If she'd been in the campground, she'd be dead.

Every bullet fired, every ping of metal against metal, reminded Esme that her family—the one she had loved and admired and been so proud of—wanted her dead.

Traitor. Benedict Arnold. Turn-tail. Judas.

Uncle Angus had whispered all those names as he tried to choke the life out of her four nights ago. The words were still ringing in her head and in her heart, mixing with the echoing sound of the automatic weapon Angus's hit men were using.

She wasn't sure what had happened to Ian and King. Either they'd run or they were biding their time, waiting for an opportunity to strike. One man against three didn't seem like good odds, and it was possible Ian was waiting for backup.

He could wait until the cows came home.

Esme was leaving.

She slithered through muddy grass and damp leaves, praying the sound of her retreat was covered by gunfire. Eventually, they'd stop shooting. When they did, her chance of escaping undetected would go from slim to none.

Who was she kidding?

It was already that. She might get out of the Everglades. She might get out of Florida. Eventually, though, Uncle Angus would find her. He had money backing him, and he had a lot riding on his ability to silence her. If she testified against Reginald, everything the two men had built—the entire crime family they'd grown—would collapse. He'd been chasing her for months, and he wouldn't give up now. Not with the trial date approaching. A few weeks, and she'd be in the courtroom, looking at her brother as she told the jury and judge what she'd seen him do.

She shuddered, sliding deeper into the foliage.

She wasn't going to give up on life, and she couldn't give up on saving the one remaining bright spot in her very dark family tree.

Violetta.

They hadn't seen or spoken to each other since Esme had gone into witness protection, but they were sisters, bound by blood and by genuine affection for each other. As far as Esme knew, Violetta hadn't been involved in any of Reginald's and Angus's crimes. Whether or not she'd known about them, however, was a question Esme needed to ask.

After she testified and shut her brother's operations down for good.

The gunfire stopped, and she froze, her belly pressed into damp earth, her heart thundering. They'd check the canoe, find it empty, realize she'd escaped.

She had to get farther away before that happened.

Taking a deep breath, she slithered forward, her pack slung over her shoulder, the soft rustle of leaves making her heart beat harder. A man called out, and someone splashed into the water, cursing loudly as he went.

She used the commotion as cover, moving quickly, trying to put as much distance between herself and the campsite as possible.

"FBI, K-9 unit. Put your weapons down or I'll release my dog," a man called, his voice carrying above the chaos.

She froze again. Ian *was* still there. She hadn't intended on spending much time with him. The entire time they'd been talking, she'd been planning her escape, trying to work out a solution to the newest problem. Just like she did when she'd planned a wedding and there was a hiccup on the big day.

"I said, drop your weapons," he repeated sharply.

A single shot rang out, and someone shouted. A dog growled, and Esme could picture the dark-eyed, dark-faced K-9 racing into danger.

Two against three.

One weapon against many.

She couldn't leave.

No matter how much she wanted to.

She couldn't abandon a man to almost certain death.

Esme didn't have a gun, but she had surprise on her side. She scooted back the way she'd come, the dog growling and barking, men shouting, chaos filling the darkness. She was heading right toward it, because she didn't know when to quit. Another thing Brent had said to her.

He'd been right.

She never quit.

Not even when the odds were stacked against her. Hopefully, this time, it wouldn't get her killed.

She crawled closer to the edge of the campsite, dropping her pack and grabbing a fist-sized rock from the mud. Reginald had taught her to play ball when they were kids. He'd shown her how to throw a mean right hook, to take a man down with a well-placed kick. She'd loved him as much as she'd loved Violetta, and she'd soaked up everything he'd had to offer. Until she'd realized that the road he'd chosen was one she had no intention of traveling. Then she'd distanced herself from her brother and, to a lesser extent, Violetta. That had been eight years ago. Even after all that time and all the years away from Reginald's coaching, she still knew how to fight.

She stopped at the edge of the clearing, her heart pounding as she waited. The campsite had gone silent. No gunfire. No barking dog. Sirens were blaring in the distance, the sound muted by the thick foliage.

Somewhere nearby, a branch snapped, the sound breaking the eerie quiet. King barked again, and someone crashed through the brush just steps from where Esme lay.

She levered up, would have lobbed the rock at the fleeing man, but King was there, a shadowy blur, so close she could feel his fur as he raced past.

Surprised, she jerked back, her knees slipping in the layer of wet earth, her elbows sliding out from under her. She would have face-planted, but someone grabbed the back of her shirt, yanking her up.

"Hey!" She turned, the rock still in her hand.

"I told you to stay where you were," Ian growled.

"I was trying to help."

"Since when is getting in the way helping?" he retorted, King's wild barking nearly covering his words.

Esme didn't think he expected a response, and she didn't bother giving one. He was already moving again, sprinting toward his dog.

She followed, keeping a few steps behind him. Despite his sarcastic comment, she had no intention of getting in the way. The more gunmen he could take out, the safer they'd be. Once they were safe, she could go back to her plan. Get out of the Everglades and out of Florida.

Alone.

"Federal agent! Freeze!" Ian shouted, and she froze before she realized he hadn't shouted the command at her.

"Call off your dog!" a man replied, his voice tinged with a hint of panic.

"You want me to call off the dog, you freeze."

"This is all a mistake!" the man whined. "I was out here hunting gators and—"

"One command, and his teeth will go straight to the bone," Ian cut in.

The man must have stopped moving, because Ian stepped forward, gun trained toward something Esme couldn't see.

"Keep your hands where I can see them," he commanded, King still growling beside him.

"And you," he continued, and even though he hadn't turned to look at her, Esme was certain he was talking to her. "Stay where you are. The guy ditched his gun back at the campsite, but that doesn't mean he's not armed."

"I ditched my gun because your crazy dog was trying to kill me."

"You can explain it all to the judge."

"What judge? I was hunting gators. I can't help it if I got in the middle of your shoot-out."

"Like I said, you can explain it all to the judge. I'm sure he'll be really interested in your version. He'll also be interested in what your friend has to say. If he survives."

"I didn't come with a friend. Never seen either of those men before in my life."

Ian didn't respond.

Esme could hear the men walking toward her, their feet slapping against wet grass and soggy leaves. They reached her seconds later, Ian taller and broader than the man he'd apprehended. He looked fit and strong. The perfect bodyguard. If she were looking for one. She wasn't. What she was looking for was some peace. She wouldn't get that until her uncle was apprehended and he and her brother were convicted of their crimes.

"What now?" she asked, trying to think ahead, to figure out the best way to separate herself from the situation. Once she knew his plans, it would be easier to make hers.

"We're heading back to the camp. I've got one man down and cuffed there. The other ran off."

"He could return," she pointed out.

"Local law enforcement is close. Hopefully, one of them will pick him up."

"I stopped hoping for safety right around the time my uncle tried to murder me," she muttered.

He eyed her through the evening gloom, his expression unreadable. For a moment, she thought he wouldn't respond. When he did, his tone was gruff. "I hope you're not living in the delusion that your uncle is the one responsible for all of this."

"Who else would it be?"

"Your uncle might have tracked you to Florida, but your brother is calling the shots from prison."

"Maybe." Probably.

She didn't want to admit that.

Not even to herself.

She and her uncle had never been close. She could almost pretend they weren't family.

She and Reginald, though…

They were siblings. Sure, he was much older, but they'd been raised by the same parents with the same values.

Somehow they'd taken completely different paths, found value in completely different things.

She'd watched him kill a man.

She would never forget that. She *would* testify against him.

But this was by far the most difficult thing she'd ever done.

It was the right thing, but that didn't make her feel good about it. It sure didn't make her safe. Her family would do anything to keep her from testifying. She still couldn't wrap her mind around that.

The proof was here, though—the cuffed man walking beside a federal agent who had come to track her down. Both of them wanted Esme for different purposes. One wanted her dead. The other wanted her to stay alive. At least until her brother's trial.

The sirens had grown louder, and she could see flashing lights through the mangroves. Help had arrived. It didn't seem like Ian needed it. He motioned for his prisoner to sit on the raised sleeping platform.

"Guard," he commanded, and King snapped to attention, his eyes trained on the cuffed man.

"He's guarding you, too," Ian said, meeting Esme's eyes.

"It's not like I have anywhere to go," she responded. She could see the canoe, a dozen yards out, listing heavily to the right. Enough bullets had been fired to cause it to sink. If she'd been in it, she'd be dead. She shivered, suddenly chilled despite the warmth and humidity.

"There are plenty of places to go. You've proved that several times." He turned and walked away, moving across the clearing and crouching next to a man who lay near the water.

She thought he was checking the guy's pulse and rendering first aid, but it was hard to see through the deepening gloom. This would have been her third night out in the Glades. She should be used to how quickly darkness descended After so many months running from people who wanted her dead, she should also be used to skin-crawling, heart-stopping fear.

The cuffed gunman shifted position, and King growled, flashing teeth that looked as deadly as any gun or knife Esme had ever seen. He was focused on the prisoner. If she were going to try to escape, now would be the time to do it. She could see the emergency vehicles, hear people moving through the mangroves. She scanned the clearing and spotted her backpack abandoned near the edge of the campsite.

It would take seconds to grab it and just a little bit longer than that to disappear. She'd done it before. She could do it again.

But she was exhausted from endless running, tired

from months of being on guard. She didn't trust the police or the FBI to keep her safe, but she wasn't sure she had the stamina to keep trying to do the job herself. Not that she had any choice.

The trial was just a month away. That seemed like forever, but it was nothing in comparison to the amount of time that had already passed. Once she testified, she'd disappear again. This time, she had no intention of being found. New name. New job. New beginning. Not the life she'd planned, but she knew she could make it a good one.

All she had to do was survive long enough to get there.

Just do it. Grab the bag and run! her mind shouted, and she was just tired enough and just scared enough to listen.

She darted forward, snagging the straps and lifting the bag in one quick motion. The rest was easy. Or should have been. The mangroves provided perfect cover, and she ducked behind one of the scrub-like trees, water lapping at her ankles as she moved.

She would have kept running, but something grabbed onto the bag, yanking her backward. She released the pack, but she was already falling, her ankle twisting as she tried to pivot and run.

She went down hard, splashing into a puddle of muck, the dog suddenly in her face, teeth bared, dark eyes staring straight into hers.

"I told you," Ian said calmly, his voice carrying through the mangroves, "he was guarding you."

She couldn't see him, and that made her almost as nervous as looking in the dog's snarling face did.

"He'd have been better off guarding the guy who

tried to kill me," she responded, not even trying to get to her feet. Not with the beast of a dog staring her down, his teeth still bared. In any other circumstance, she'd have admired him for what he was—a handsome, fit working dog. Right now, she just wanted him gone.

"The perpetrator is in police custody. I guess you were too busy planning your escape to notice them moving in."

"I noticed."

"And did you think I wouldn't notice you leaving?" Branches rustled, and he stepped into view, his head and shoulders bowed as he walked through the trees.

"What I thought was that I wanted to live, and that being alone seemed like the safest way to make sure that happened."

"Esme, you really need to stop fighting me," he said, crouching a few feet away and looking straight into her eyes. There was something about his face—the angle of his jaw, the sharp cut of his cheekbones—that made her think of the old Westerns she used to watch with her dad, the hero cowboy riding to the rescue on his trusty steed. Only, this hero didn't have a horse; he had a dog.

"I'm not. I'm making your job easier. Go back to your office and tell anyone who cares that I refused federal help. I want to do this alone."

"What? Get yourself killed?"

"Call off your dog, okay? I want to get out of the mud." And the Everglades and the mess her family had created.

To her surprise, he complied.

"Release!" he said, and the dog backed off, sitting on his haunches, still watching her. Only this time, she was sure he was grinning.

* * *

King had had a great night. He'd found his mark twice and brought in an armed man. He was obviously pleased with himself, his tail splashing in a puddle of water, his dark eyes turned up to Ian.

"Good boy," Ian said, scratching behind King's ears and offering the praise he'd been waiting for.

"That's a matter of opinion," Esme muttered.

Ian flashed his light in her direction. She'd fallen hard but didn't seem to be much worse for the wear. "He did what I asked him to. That's always a win."

"That depends on what side of his teeth you're sitting on."

"He wasn't going to bite you."

"Right," she scoffed, tucking a strand of auburn hair behind her ear. She hadn't colored it. That had surprised him. It would have been the first thing he'd have done if he'd been in her position.

"He bites when he has to, but it's not in his nature to snap. Unless I give him the command."

"I'll keep that in mind," she said, a hint of weariness in her voice. She looked as exhausted as she sounded—her skin paper white in the twilight, dark circles beneath her eyes. He'd seen photos of her taken just a few months before she'd watched her brother execute a man. Her cheeks hadn't been as hollow, her shoulders as narrow.

He didn't want to feel sorry for her. She was, after all, part of the family that had taken his. Years ago, Reginald Dupree had called the hit on Ian's father. He'd been just starting out, sticking his toes in the water of his new family business. Ian's father had been a Chicago police officer, determined to undermine Dupree's efforts. He'd arrested two of Reginald's lower-level operatives. In retaliation, Reginald had paid a couple of street thugs to shoot him when he left the house for work. They'd opened fire as he'd stepped outside. The first bullet had killed him instantly. The second had killed Ian's mother, who'd been standing in the doorway saying goodbye.

Yeah. He didn't want to feel sorry for anyone in the family, but his father had raised him to be compassionate, to look out for those who couldn't look out for themselves. More than that, he'd raised him to do what was right. Even when it was difficult. The right thing to do was to protect Esme. Despite her last name and her family, she'd committed no crime.

"How about you keep something else in mind, too?" He offered a hand, and she allowed him to pull her to her feet.

"What?"

"Next time I tell you to stay somewhere, you should do it. It's a waste of King's energy to chase after you when he's supposed to be keeping you safe."

"You told him to guard me," she pointed out.

"Because the closer you are, the easier it is for me to make sure your brother doesn't get what he wants."

"Me dead, you mean?"

"I wasn't going to put it so bluntly, but yes."

"My uncle is the one who wants me dead, Ian. It's his hands that were around my throat the other night." Her tone was hard, her voice raspy, and the compassion he didn't want to feel welled up again.

"Does it make you feel better to keep telling yourself that?" he asked gently.

"It will make me feel better to be done with this. It

will make me feel better to do what I promised and to get on with my life. So how about you leave me alone and let me go back to the business of staying safe until the trial?"

"Do you think this will all end if we have your uncle in custody?" he asked, calling King to heel and leading Esme back the way they'd come.

"I hope it will," she murmured, limping as she tried to keep pace with him. She must have hurt her leg or foot. He shouldn't have cared. She was a means to an end. Despite the clean criminal record, the supposedly upright business, she was who she was—a Dupree.

But he did care, because she was a person who'd found herself in an untenable position and had chosen to do the right thing. She'd witnessed a horrible crime, and despite the fact that her brother had committed it, she'd gone to the police and offered to testify.

"What'd you do to your leg?" he asked, and she shrugged.

"Twisted my ankle. It's fine."

"Then why are you limping?"

"Because I'm tired, okay? Because I want to get out of this stupid swamp and into clean clothes. I want to take a shower and wash three days' worth of bug repellent off my skin. Mostly, I just want to close my eyes, open them and find out that this has all been some horrible nightmare."

"I'm sorry," he said and meant it.

"For what? Being the one they chose for this assignment?"

"For the fact that all of this isn't just a bad dream. Your family has deep pockets, Esme. They can afford to pay people to do their dirty work. Which means you won't be safe until we shut down the crime ring your brother and uncle control."

"You're a wellspring of joyful tidings, Ian."

"I'm honest."

"And, like I said, I'm tired. So how about we discuss this another time?"

"You want to survive, right?" He stopped short and looked straight into her pale face.

"Would I have spent three days in the Everglades if I didn't?"

"Some people love it here."

"I'm not one of them," she huffed.

"And yet, this is where you ran when you left witness protection."

"My parents and I spent every summer here when I was a kid. They're—"

"Buried twenty miles from here. I know. I'm sure your uncle knew. Your brother. Your sister."

"I feel like you're trying to make a point, so how about you just get to it?" Her hands were on her hips, her chin raised. Of the three Dupree siblings, she was the one Ian understood the least. Reginald was all about power and money. He'd go to any length to get it. Violetta wanted the same, but she wasn't willing to break the law to get it. On the other hand, she wasn't willing to cooperate with law enforcement to make her brother pay for his crimes.

But Esme…

Ian couldn't wrap her in a tidy package and put a label on her. That bothered him. He'd spent most of his adult life studying people, figuring them out, deciding whether they were telling the truth, were dangerous or could be trusted. He'd missed the mark with Jake Morrow. A member of the Tactical K-9 team, Jake had put on a good show. He'd pretended to be everything the team believed in—a man of honesty, integrity, honor. That hadn't meant Ian had liked him. There'd always been something a little cocky about Jake, something a little off. Still, he'd trusted him.

That trust had been misplaced.

Jake had been on the Dupree payroll. He'd betrayed the team, and he was still on the loose, still causing trouble.

"Here's my point," he said, King panting quietly beside him. "You came to a place where anyone who knew anything about you would look for you. You would have been better off sticking with witness protection."

"One innocent person already lost her life because I was in the program. I'm not going to risk someone else dying for the same reason."

"We had a leak. We've sealed it. No one else is going to be hurt," he responded, keeping his tone neutral. He'd thought she was worried about her own safety, that she'd run from the program because she thought she'd be safer away from it. The fact that she'd been worried about others put a twist on things. A twist he didn't like. He wanted to lump her in with the rest of the family, but no matter how hard he tried, he couldn't seem to do it.

"You don't seem to understand." She swung around, her auburn ponytail flying in an arc as she moved. "One person being hurt is too many. I think about it every day. About how that woman died because someone mistook her for me."

"It wasn't because of you. It was because of your uncle and your brother. It was because they thought they were above the law, because they hadn't expected to ever be stopped. They like their money and their power, and neither of them want to give it up."

"Yeah. I know." She sighed, walking away, heading toward the distant emergency lights, her stride hitched but brisk, her shoulders straight.

"Esme," he said, not sure what he wanted to add, what he could possibly say to make things better or easier or right.

"I think we've both said everything we need to, Ian. How about you just let me do what I need to? I'm sure the police would like to talk to you, and I've got a long way to go before I reach civilization."

He could have stopped her.

He had the authority to do it. He had the strength. He had King.

But he let her go, because he thought she needed some space. It was five miles to the main road, and there were emergency vehicles everywhere. She'd be safe enough.

"All right," he said, and she met his eyes.

He thought he saw tears before she looked away again.

Then she was moving, putting distance between them, her backpack lying a yard away, abandoned on the muddy ground. He snagged it, figuring she'd want it later. He needed to check in with the local police, and then he'd get in his SUV and pick her up on the way out.

"King," he said, and the dog looked at him, eager for the next command. "Guard!"

The Malinois took off, racing across the clearing, his light brown fur visible in the darkness as he followed Esme through the trees and out into the main campground.

THREE

Long Pine Key Campground was not difficult to find. Esme simply followed the flashing emergency lights through a copse of mangroves and out into a field of vegetation. The vehicles were probably a quarter mile away, but the darkness made them easy enough to see. She picked her way across the field, the ground growing soggier with every step. If it got any wetter, she'd have to find another route. She didn't mind getting wet, but she didn't like the idea of being knee-deep in water that was filled with slimy, slithery, scaly creatures.

Esme was almost ready to turn back when she spotted a wooden walkway that stretched the remainder of the way across the area. She stepped onto it, the wood giving a little as she moved.

She was halfway over when she heard quiet panting and the soft pad of paws. Her heart in her throat, she spun around, her sore ankle nearly giving out. The dog was there. Of course. *King.* And he was so close she could have reached out and touched his nose, so close she could feel his panting breath on her hand, see his goofy smile through the darkness.

Because he was smiling again.

Why wouldn't he be?

She kept running. He kept finding her. A fun game for a dog. Not so much fun for Esme.

"Go home," she commanded.

The dog didn't even blink.

"Where's your partner?" She glanced back the way she'd come, saw nothing but the empty field and shadowy mangroves. "Did he tell you to follow me?"

The dog settled on his haunches, his dark eyes looking straight into hers.

"Release!" she commanded, pointing in the direction she wanted him to go.

Nothing.

"Go! Cease!"

Still nothing.

"Fine. Do what you want. I've got more important things to do than argue with a dog." She limped the rest of the way across the boardwalk, stepping onto wet grass, King close behind her.

The Long Pine Key parking area was straight ahead, the dark figures of emergency personnel visible in the flashing strobe lights of their vehicles. She'd seen way too many emergency vehicles the past few months. Beginning with the one that had been sent to the scene of her brother's crime.

She'd still been in shock—the memory of Reginald pointing the gun and firing it, of a man falling to the ground, blood spurting from his chest, taking up so much room in her mind, there hadn't been space to create memories of conversations she'd had, of people she'd spoken to. All she could remember were the emergency lights and the questions, barked one right after another—a series of words that had had no meaning.

Esme sighed.

She knew Ian meant well. She knew the FBI meant well. Law enforcement, witness protection, they meant well, too. But meaning well couldn't keep her alive.

Better to not take a chance of being waylaid by another well-meaning entity. She'd steer clear of law enforcement. She turned to the right, heading through a grove of cypress trees, aiming for the road that led into the parking lot. It should be straight ahead. She didn't have her map, but she'd memorized the topography and knew what landmarks to look for to ascertain how far she was from civilization. It would be a long walk to anyplace where she could make a phone call. Five miles on the back road, then out onto a main road that would eventually lead her to town. Once there, she'd borrow a phone and call…

Who?

Not Violetta. She loved her sister, but she couldn't count on her. Not the way she'd thought she could. Violetta's loyalties were torn. She wanted to support Reginald and see him freed from prison. Esme knew that, and she knew why. It wasn't all about love and family. At least not according to the FBI, it wasn't. Violetta had been happy to take whatever gifts Reginald offered—money for a new car, financial backing to support her business, new windows for her house. Esme had been shown a list of all the things her sister had accepted from Reginald.

At first, she'd argued that Violetta hadn't known where Reginald was getting the money. But, of course, the FBI had been prepared for that. They'd proved her wrong. Violetta *had* known…she just hadn't cared. She'd kept her hands clean, but she sure hadn't been willing to jeopardize Reginald's *career*. After all, she was benefiting too much from it.

The last time Esme had seen her sister had been six months ago. Violetta had looked just as cool and reserved as ever, her beautiful face not showing even a hint of stress or anxiety. Esme, on the other hand, had been a mess. But, then, she was the one who'd watched a man die. She was the one who'd had to make a choice between family and justice. She was the one who was swimming against the tide and doing exactly what her family didn't want her to.

And she was the one who'd pay with her life if her uncle got his hands on her again.

Esme shuddered, her skin clammy from the humid air, her body leaden from too many restless nights. She had to believe that she was going to get through this. She had to trust that God would keep her safe, that doing the right thing would always be best even when it felt so horribly wrong.

Betrayer. Traitor. Turncoat.

Her uncle's words were still in her head, the feel of his fingers around her throat enough to make her want to gag. She stumbled, tripping over a root and going down hard, her hands and knees sliding across damp earth, her shoulder bumping into a tree trunk.

She lay where she was for a few minutes too long, the muted sound of voices carrying on the still night air. Maybe she should go to the parking lot, turn herself in to the authorities and hope and pray that they could keep her safe. That seemed so much easier than going it alone.

It also seemed more dangerous.

A woman had died, and she'd almost been killed

because of an information leak. Ian had told her the leak had been plugged, but she couldn't count on that. She couldn't really count on anything.

"Your pity party is getting you nowhere," she muttered, pushing up onto her hands and knees.

A cool wet nose pressed against her cheek, and King huffed quietly. She jerked back, looking into his dark face. He was a handsome dog when he wasn't snarling and showing teeth. Right now, he looked like he was smiling again, his tongue lolling out to the side.

"I think I told you to find your partner," she scolded, forcing herself up. Lying around feeling sorry for herself would accomplish absolutely nothing. Going back into the situation that had almost gotten her killed would do the same.

She had to stay the course—find a place to go to ground until trial, then contact the authorities and arrange to be escorted to court. Armed guards would be great. Six or seven dogs like King would be a nice bonus.

Right now, though...

Right now, she just had to find a safe place to hide.

She started walking again, trudging through saw grass and heading away from the emergency vehicles. There were no streetlights on the road, no beacons to lead her in the right direction. She went by instinct, the rising moon giving her at least some idea of what direction she was heading.

Northeast would bring her to the road.

The road would bring her to civilization.

She'd figure out everything else once she got there.

The grass opened up, the earth dried out and she could see the road winding snakelike through the Everglades. She stepped onto it, her ankle throbbing, her stomach churning. After three days and nights in the Everglades, it felt strange to be out in the open. No water surrounding her. No foliage to shelter in. She could see emergency lights to the left, so she turned right, trudging along the road as if she didn't have a care in the world.

Five miles wasn't much.

She loved hiking, biking and running. Before she'd entered witness protection, she'd been training for a half marathon. Walking a few miles should have been a piece of cake, but she felt like she was slogging through mud, her legs heavy with fatigue.

King pressed close to her leg, his shoulder brushing her thigh as they walked. He didn't look nervous, and she took that as a good sign. It wasn't good that he was sticking to her like glue, however, because eventually his handler would come looking for him. When he did, he'd find Esme, too.

Unless Esme could ditch the dog.

She patted the pockets of her cargo pants, found the package of peanut butter crackers she'd planned to eat for dinner. She opened it, the rustling paper not even garnering a glance from King.

She slipped a cracker from the sleeve, held it out to the dog. "Hungry?" she asked.

He ignored her and the cracker.

"King?" She nudged the cracker close to his mouth.

He didn't break his stride, didn't look at the food.

"It's peanut butter. Peanut butter is good. Fetch!" She waved it closer to his face, then threw it back in the direction they'd come.

It hit the pavement, and King just kept walking.

Esme blew out a frustrated breath. Great...just great. Now she'd end up in town with a dog that didn't belong to her. Probably a very expensive dog. The FBI wouldn't be happy if she left the state with one of their dogs in tow.

For all she knew, she'd be charged with kidnapping.

Dognapping?

"King!" she said, trying to put an edge of command in her voice. "Sit!"

He didn't.

"Fetch!" She tried another cracker. "Retrieve!"

"Do you not speak English?" she asked, stopping short and eyeing the dog. He was still wearing his vest, a logo on the side announcing that he was a law enforcement dog. Esme wasn't sure about much lately, but she knew this—she did not look like a law enforcement officer. At least not one that was on duty. She didn't have a uniform, a gun or a holster. And no badge. If she made it to town, people would wonder what she was doing with a dog who was obviously supposed to be working.

"This is a problem," she said, crouching a few feet from the dog and watching him. He was watching her just as steadily.

"Listen, buddy, I'm sure your handler told you to follow me, but I'd prefer you go back to what you were doing before you got sent on this wild-goose chase."

He cocked his head to the side, then glanced back the way they'd come. He'd gone from alert to stiff with tension. She wasn't sure what that meant, but it couldn't be anything good.

"What is it?" she whispered, as if the dog could answer.

He barked once—a quick high-pitched sound that made her hair stand on end.

Someone or something was coming.

That was the only explanation.

She ran to the side of the road, plunging into the thick shrubs that lined it. She didn't know if King had followed. She was too focused on finding a place to hide. She crouched low, her heart throbbing hollowly in her ears. Lights splashed across the road and filtered through the leaves.

A car was coming. First the headlights, then the soft chug of an engine. She shrank deeper into the shadows, King's lean body suddenly beside her, pressing in so close his fur rubbed against her arm. Mosquitoes buzzed, dive-bombing the exposed areas of Esme's skin. She didn't dare swat them away. The car was closing in, the engine growing louder. She wanted to grab King's collar and make sure he didn't lunge out from their hiding place, but she couldn't get the image of him barking at the gunmen out of her head. No matter how hard she tried, she couldn't stop seeing his sharp teeth and snarling mouth. Sure, he currently looked like a sweet goofy pet, but she knew he could be vicious if he needed to be. She'd keep her hands to herself and hope for the best rather than risk losing one of her fingers to his sharp teeth.

"Don't move," she whispered, and the dog shifted closer, his shoulder leaning into hers.

The car slowed as it approached, the tires rolling over dry pavement.

Keep going, she silently commanded. *Please, keep going.*

The car stopped, the engine idling, the soft chug making her blood run cold. Could the driver see her? Did he know she was there?

A door opened, and she stiffened. She had no weapon.

Her only option was to run. In a place as inhospitable as the Everglades, that could get a person killed.

Staying could get her killed, too.

She waited another minute, praying that whoever was on the road had stopped to look at a snake or save a turtle or do some completely normal thing that didn't involve hunting a woman through the swamp.

King barked, the sound so loud and startling, Esme jumped.

She didn't scream, but she came close.

And then she ran, darting away from the road as fast as her twisted ankle could carry her.

Two strides and Ian caught up, catching Esme's arm before she could run any farther.

She swung around, throwing a punch that nearly hit its mark.

"Hey! Cool it," he growled, dragging her arm down to her side the same way he had before. This time there was no knife, and she looked even more scared, her eyes wild with fear.

"Let me go!" she demanded, and he did, releasing his hold and stepping back.

"Calm down, Esme. It's just me."

She met his eyes, seemed to finally realize who he was and frowned. "You just scared six years off my life."

"Sorry about that."

"You don't sound sorry," she accused.

"Maybe because I'm tired of following you all over Florida," he replied, and she cracked a half smile.

"I'm not going to apologize, if that's what you're hoping for."

"I'm hoping we can get out of this area before we

run into more trouble." He took her hand again, and this time, she didn't resist as he led her back to the road and his SUV.

He opened the back hatch and called for King, and she didn't say a word, didn't try to leave.

The Malinois jumped in, settling into his kennel and heaving a sigh that would have made Ian smile if he hadn't been standing next to Esme.

She was a problem.

Up until he'd tracked her down, he'd been resentful of the time and resources they were putting into finding her. The prosecutor had a good case against Reginald Dupree—even without his sister's testimony. She was the witness who would put him away for good, though. First-degree murder. Planned and executed with cunning and without remorse.

Esme was the only witness, and without her testimony, evidence was circumstantial at best. At worst, it was unconvincing. A good defense lawyer might get Reginald off. That wasn't something Ian was going to allow.

Yeah. He'd wanted to keep her safe for purely mercenary purposes. With her testimony, the Dupree crime family could be stopped. Without it, Reginald might go free.

Now…

He was beginning to feel sorry for her, beginning to see her as something other than the family she'd been born into. She'd given up her entire life to make sure her brother went to jail for his crime. She'd left her job, her friends, her fiancé. She'd done it all without complaining. Everyone who'd met her or worked with her had had only good things to say.

He'd told himself it was because she was a good actress and consummate manipulator. After hearing her talk about the woman who'd died, hearing the regret in her voice, seeing the tears in her eyes, he doubted that was the case.

Unless he was misreading her, she was who everyone else on the team seemed to think she was—a woman who'd been pulled into something she hadn't expected or wanted. A woman who'd been running from her family because she valued doing what was right more than she valued loyalty to her family.

A tough place to be standing.

A tough decision to make.

She'd made it. She'd continued to say that she would testify despite the obvious threats against her.

He admired that.

A lot.

He frowned, closing the back hatch and turning to face Esme. "Did you really think you were going to walk out of here?"

"I sure didn't think I wasn't going to," she replied, flipping her ponytail over her shoulder. A few strands of hair had escaped and were clinging to her throat and neck, the dark red strands gleaming in the SUV's parking lights.

"The nearest town is twenty miles away," he pointed out.

"I've walked farther."

"Did you do it when you had a price on your head?"

She pressed her lips together and didn't say a word.

"I'll take that as a no." He led her to the passenger side of the vehicle. "You keep walking on this road, and someone else is going to find you. If it happens to be one of your uncle's hired guns, you don't have a chance of surviving."

"I'm not sure my chances are any higher with you," she responded, but she didn't walk away.

Maybe she was too tired.

Maybe the injury to her ankle was worse than she'd been letting on.

Whatever the case, she stayed right where she was as he opened the door.

"How about we discuss it on the way to the local police department?"

"Ian…" She shook her head. "I believed your organization when I was told I'd be safe. They were wrong, and I can't see any reason to believe you again."

"And yet you're still standing here."

"Because I'm tired. I've been running for months, and I have at least another month to go before the trial. It's hard to sleep when you're worried someone is going to break in and kill you. Without sleep, it's really difficult to make good decisions."

Her honesty surprised him, and he touched her arm, urging her to the open door. "I've had plenty of sleep. How about you let me make the decisions for a while?"

She laughed without humor. "You're very convincing, but I think I'll pass."

"Then how about you sit in the SUV while I drive, and spend a little time thinking about what you want to do? It'll be easier doing it in a safe place than it will while you're out in the open."

"Like I said," she responded, finally stepping away. "You're convincing, but I'm going to have to pass."

"You're a long way from the state line, Esme."

"I was a long way from Florida a couple of months

ago. Now I'm here, and eventually I'll be somewhere else."

"You agreed to testify," he said, trying a different tactic. She was coming with him. There could be no other outcome, but he'd like her to think she'd been the one to make the decision.

"I will testify."

"That's going to be difficult to do if you're off the grid and have no contact with us."

"Just because you can't find me, doesn't mean I won't be able to find you. I'll be at the trial." A note of weary resignation laced her tone. "I'll provide testimony that will put my brother in jail for the rest of his life."

"If you don't—"

"I know what will happen if I don't. I'll die. I may die anyway, but that's okay, right? A member of the Dupree crime family dies, and no one in a uniform is going to mourn." She started walking again, the limp more pronounced.

"You're not going to get very far with an injured leg."

"Ankle," she responded. "And I'll get wherever I want to go. Just let me, okay? Tell your boss and your team and the prosecuting attorney that I refused your help."

"I can't." That was the truth. He'd sworn to uphold the law. Just like his father and grandfather and great-grandfather, he'd always known he was going to be a cop. He'd worked the beat in Chicago, just like three generations of Slades had. And then he'd reached further, applying to the FBI, passing the physicals, the tests, the interviews.

His father would have been proud of him.

If he'd lived long enough to see it.

"Why? Because I signed some papers that said I agreed to witness protection?" Esme asked.

"Because you're more vulnerable than you want to think you are," he told her. "Because you're injured and you need to see a doctor. Because your backpack is in my vehicle, and without it, you've got nothing."

She hesitated, her gaze darting to the Suburban.

"It would be a lot easier for you to get where you're going with that pack, right?" he continued, certain he'd finally found the key to getting her to cooperate.

"Right," she agreed. "So how about you give it to me, and we can both be on our way?"

"How about I get you checked out at the hospital, and then I give it to you?"

"Are you bribing me to get me to cooperate?" she demanded.

"Yes," he responded, turning back to the SUV, and to his surprise, she followed. He helped her into the passenger seat and closed the door.

She was probably hoping to grab the pack and run, but he'd tucked it in next to King's crate. She'd have to reach over the backseat to do it.

That would take time, and he didn't plan to give her that.

He jogged around to the driver's side and climbed in. She was already on her knees, reaching into the back.

"Don't," he said, locking the doors and putting the vehicle into Drive.

"What?"

"Keep trying to run. It almost got you killed twice. The third time, you might not survive."

Pursing her lips, she settled into the seat, yanked her seat belt across her lap and didn't say another word. Her silence shouldn't have bothered him. As a matter of fact, he should have preferred it over conversation. She was an assignment, a job he'd been asked to take and that he'd accepted. No matter how much he hadn't wanted to.

He'd been after the Duprees since his parents' murders. He and his team were this close to shutting them down.

Esme was a means to an end, but she was also a human being. One who'd been through a lot. One who deserved as much peace and security as he could offer her.

She shivered, pulling her hands up into the cuffs of her jacket. It had been hot the past few days, but she'd dressed to keep the bugs away—long pants, jacket, boots.

"Cold?" he asked, and she shook her head.

He turned on the heat anyway, blasting it into the already warm vehicle, wishing he could do more for her. Wanting to break the silence and tell her everything was going to be okay.

She wouldn't believe him if he did, so he stayed silent.

He wanted to think Esme had resigned herself to staying in protective custody. However, based on the fact that she'd spent the past few months on the run, he couldn't.

He dialed his boss, waiting impatiently for Max West to pick up. They'd spoken a few weeks ago, and Max had made it clear that he trusted Ian to do the job he'd been assigned.

Ian hadn't been pleased with the conversation. His past was his business, and he liked to keep it that way. The fact that Max knew about his parents' murders didn't surprise him. The fact that he'd brought it up had. The fact that he'd flat-out told Ian that he needed to focus on justice and forget about revenge?

That still stung.

Sure, Ian wanted to put an end to the crime family.

Sure, he wanted to avenge his parents' murders.

Justice always came first, though. That was the goal. The joy of seeing his parents' murderer sent to jail forever would simply be the bonus shot.

"West here." The team captain's voice cut through the silence. "You have her?"

"Word travels fast," Ian mused, his attention on the dark road that stretched out in front of him.

"It does when it involves one of the Duprees."

Esme tensed.

"You're on speakerphone, and she's in the vehicle," Ian cautioned.

"How are you doing, Ms. Dupree?" Max asked.

"I'd be better if your organization would leave me alone."

"I'm sure you know that's not possible until after the trial."

"You're assuming I'll make it to trial, but at the rate things are going, that doesn't seem likely."

"There's nothing to worry about. We've got things under control."

She laughed, the sound harsh and tight. "Like you did a few months ago when I agreed to enter the program?"

"Ms. Dupree—"

"How about we hash this out once I have her in a safe location?" Ian cut in.

"You're going to try to bring her to headquarters, right?" Max asked. "She'll be safer here than anywhere else."

"You think that's wise? Jake knows the setup there. He knows the security strengths and weaknesses." Jake Morrow had disappeared months ago. At first the team had assumed he'd been killed or abducted by the Duprees. The truth was a lot harder to swallow. He'd gone rogue and was feeding information to the crime family.

"You've got a point," Max said. "Tell you what. I'll see if we have a safe house available somewhere close to you. Once I locate one, I'll send a couple team members down to help with guard duty."

"I don't need to be guarded," Esme cut in.

"That sounds good," he said, ignoring her protest.

She'd agreed to enter the witness protection program, which meant she'd agreed to following the rules set up to protect her.

She was going to stick by those agreements whether she liked it or not.

And maybe, while she was at it, she could point the way to her uncle. Angus Dupree had been free for too long.

Ian wanted him behind bars.

Once that was accomplished, the Dupree crime family would be defunct. That was his personal goal, and it was the best revenge.

"Give me a half hour and I should have something set up," Max said. "Where are you headed now?"

"The regional hospital. Esme injured her ankle. We're getting it checked out."

"That's Big Cypress Regional Medical Center?" Max asked, probably staring at a map of the area, trying to figure out the easiest route there, as well as to the closest safe house.

"Right."

"I'll call for some local manpower. Angus is probably still in the area. He's smart. He's quick. He's not going to give up easily."

"He's not going to give up until I'm dead," Esme murmured.

"Or until he's behind bars," Ian added.

"That's the goal," Max said. "What's your ETA for the hospital?"

"Twenty-five minutes."

"We'll have someone there to meet you." Max disconnected, and the SUV fell silent.

Ian could have broken the silence.

He could have offered more reassurances, made a few more promises about keeping her safe. If she'd been anyone else, he probably would have. But Esme was a Dupree, and he was a man whose family had been brutally murdered by hers.

He needed to keep that in mind.

Because he couldn't afford to have too much compassion for her. He couldn't afford to let himself see her as more than just the sister of the man he wanted to destroy.

He scowled.

Destroy was a harsh word. It was the kind of word that, if spoken aloud, would make other people think he was out for revenge. Maybe he was. Maybe that really was what this was all about. Maybe Max had been right to call him on it.

In the end, though, he'd follow protocol. He'd use the law to get what he wanted.

And Esme?

She was part of that. An enemy by association.

Whether she knew it or not.

FOUR

The hospital was little more than a small clinic sitting at the edge of a tiny town. One story. Brick. Probably built in the early seventies. There was a main entrance in the front, and Esme assumed there were several other doors around the sides and back. She could see two police cruisers parked near the curb, lights flashing brightly in the darkness.

If that was the manpower Ian's boss had called in, she shouldn't have any difficulty escaping again. Once she had her backpack.

She waited impatiently as Ian opened the back hatch and attached King to a lead. Ian had been silent for most of the drive, and she hadn't bothered trying to make conversation.

She hadn't wanted to discuss her family and what they were capable of. She hadn't wanted to rehash the same tired conversation she'd had every time she'd spoken to a federal agent. They wanted to remind her of the crimes her brother and uncle had committed. They didn't want her to forget her obligations.

She'd been surprised that Ian hadn't done either of those things. His silence had been a welcome relief, the heat that he'd turned on for her chasing away the chill that she shouldn't have been feeling.

It was nearly ninety degrees outside, but she'd still been cold.

He'd noticed, and that shouldn't have mattered to her, but it had. It had been weeks since she'd had another human being around, months since she'd spoken to any of her friends. She'd never known loneliness before. Now it seemed it was all she had.

One day, one night, after another.

Just Esme and her thoughts, alone in whatever squalid little dive she could rent for cheap.

Her door opened, and Ian leaned down, met her eyes. "Do you want me to get a wheelchair?"

"I'm okay."

"No," he responded, his voice much kinder than she'd expected or wanted. "You're not. But you will be. Eventually."

And for some reason, that made her throat tighten and her eyes burn. It made her want to cry all the tears she hadn't cried in the weeks after she'd entered witness protection.

He offered a hand, and she took it, allowing herself to be pulled from the vehicle. He had her pack over his arm, and she reached for it. "I can take that."

"I've got it," he responded, shifting his hand to her elbow, his palm warm through her thin jacket.

"I'm not so badly hurt that I can't carry my own pack and walk unassisted," she muttered.

"I wouldn't want you to injure your ankle more."

Right. Sure. The way she saw things, he was probably trying to keep her from running.

It still felt good to have someone nearby, though.

She hated to admit that.

She hated that she was enjoying the warmth of his hand, the comfort of his company.

She'd been part of a couple for so long, it had felt strange to not be. To wake up in the morning knowing she wouldn't need to call Brent, text him, wish him good morning or ask him about his day.

He could have entered witness protection with her.

They could have gotten married and made a new life together. Maybe they would have, if Brent hadn't been so adamant about staying in Chicago. He'd made certain that she knew that he wasn't going to follow her into witness protection, that he wouldn't give up his life and his friends and his church group to be with her while she waited to testify. He'd also made certain she'd understood that he wouldn't be waiting for her. That if she went into witness protection, they were over. The wedding they'd been planning, the one that they'd sent out invitations for, that she'd bought a gown for, that she had a venue and flowers and cake for, wouldn't be happening.

If you leave, we're done, he'd said, and she'd almost thought he was joking. They'd been standing in a small conference room at FBI headquarters in Chicago, and she'd been given the offer of protection in exchange for her testimony. Six months wasn't that long. Not for two people who were in love. Well, apparently, she and Brent *hadn't* been in love, because he'd told her that six months apart was too much to ask.

For a split second, she'd considered suggesting that they move the wedding up, get married by a justice of the peace and go into the program together.

But then she'd thought better of it, because she hadn't

wanted to spend her life with a man who hadn't been willing to sacrifice a little time, a little convenience, a little of his own desires to help her do what she knew was right.

The FBI didn't know any of that.

They didn't care.

Faux concern about her ankle wouldn't make her think they did.

She reached the double doors that led into the clinic and opened them, limping into the air-conditioned lobby. After days of being out in the heat and humidity, it felt like she'd walked into an icebox. Her teeth were chattering, her arms covered in goose bumps as she approached the receptionist.

Her wallet was in the backpack. Along with her ID, her insurance card and her cash. Not just one ID. Several. The real her. The person she'd been in witness protection. The woman she'd become when she'd run.

"Sign in. We'll call you back shortly," the receptionist said, barely looking up from her computer.

She signed her real name—there didn't seem to be a whole lot of reason to do anything else. Angus knew she was in the area, but he didn't know she was injured, had no way of knowing she'd come to the hospital. Plus, he wasn't a fool. He wouldn't come after her when there were so many police around. He'd wait for a time when she was on her own again.

She rubbed the chill from her arms and settled into a chair. She thought Ian would follow, but he walked to the reception desk, leaning down and saying something that Esme couldn't hear. He took out his wallet, flashed what she assumed was his badge and jotted something on the sign-in sheet.

The receptionist eyed him as he turned away. She looked surprised and interested. Maybe because of the dog or whatever Ian had told her. Maybe because of him. He was a good-looking guy.

Better than good-looking. Dark hair. Light brown eyes. Tall and muscular. He looked like the kind of guy who could handle whatever came his way. The kind who could be depended on, who could fight his battles and everyone else's.

He must have sensed her gaze, because he met her eyes, offered a smile that made her heart flutter.

Fatigue was getting the best of her.

That much was obvious.

He crossed the room and sat beside her, his gun holster peeking out from beneath his jacket. "It shouldn't be long," he said.

"I'm not in a hurry."

"I am. This is a calculated risk. The likelihood that Angus will show up here is slim. We've got police watching all the entrances, but I'd rather be in and out quickly."

"We can skip it altogether, if you want," she said.

"I'd prefer you have the ankle looked at now rather than later. Once we get you to the safe house, you'll be sticking pretty close to it until the trial."

"So, basically, I'll be under house arrest?" she asked, not quite able to keep the sarcasm from her voice.

"Whatever keeps you safe, Esme," he responded.

"Whatever gets me to trial," she corrected.

"That, too."

She had nothing to say to that, and she found herself looking in his eyes again, studying his face. He had long lashes, and the beginning of a beard and mustache.

Clothes caked with mud and muck from the swamp, he was still one of the handsomest men she'd ever seen.

The fact that she was noticing didn't make her happy.

He looked about as annoyed as she felt. She couldn't blame him. He'd been assigned bodyguard duty. That meant hanging out and chilling, waiting for Uncle Angus's next move. It also meant giving up free time and hours that he could have been home with the people he loved.

"Just so you know, that's important to me, too," she said quietly, and he nodded, some of his annoyance seeming to melt away.

"I get that. I also understand that it's not fun having people come in and take over your life, but in this case, it's necessary."

"I'm sure it's not fun giving up your life to help protect a stranger. Your family—"

"Is gone," he bit the words out. "I have an aloe vera plant waiting for me at home, so I'm not all that concerned about my time away."

"You get lots of sunburns?"

He raised an eyebrow, and she blushed.

Blushed!

"It was a gift from a friend," he finally said, "who felt I needed something to take care of. That was in the years prior to King." He scratched the dog behind his ears.

"I see."

"Probably not, but we don't know each other well enough for a long explanation."

"Or for you to go back to the exam room with me," she pointed out, taking the opportunity that was presented to her.

"I'm going." The answer was simple, to the point and firm.

"That's not the way I do things," she responded, using her reasonable voice. The one she used with hysterical brides or overbearing mothers of the brides.

"It's the way my team does things, so it's the way it's going to be."

"Your team? Meaning the FBI?"

"Partly."

"Can you give me a plain answer, Ian, because I'm in no mood for riddles."

"No riddle. I work for a covert unit within the FBI. Our job is to take on cases like yours."

"Cases where witness protection nearly got someone killed?" she asked, and his lips curved into what she could only assume was a smile. Since there wasn't a bit of humor in his eyes, she couldn't be certain of that.

"Tough cases. Dangerous ones," he offered.

"Oh joy," she muttered.

This time, he really did smile. "Sarcasm?"

"How'd you guess?"

He chuckled. "You're an interesting lady, Esme."

"I plan people's weddings for a living. I go to church on Sunday and out to the movies every couple of months. There is nothing interesting about me."

"The federal government would beg to differ. To us, you are exceedingly interesting."

"Tell me how to change that, and I will. Hiding from my uncle would be a lot less complicated if I weren't also hiding from your people."

"Testify at the trial. Our interest in you will end at that point."

She rolled her eyes. "At least you're honest."

"About?"

"The fact that your organization will only care about me until then. Once I testify, I'll be on my own. If my uncle or my brother or anyone either of them is affiliated with comes after me, it won't be your concern."

He frowned but didn't deny it.

So, he *was* honest.

Which was nice, but didn't do much to make her feel better about the situation.

The door that led to the exam rooms opened and a dark-haired man stepped into the lobby. He glanced at a clipboard, scanned the room and finally called, "Esme Dupree?" as if she weren't the only woman there.

"Yes." She stood, Ian and King doing the same.

Ian had said he'd go into the exam room with her.

She wasn't going to argue. She wanted the pack, and it was currently hanging loosely from his left arm. Eventually, he'd relax enough to set it down.

"I'm Ryan. The PA on duty tonight. You said you injured your ankle?" The man glanced down as he spoke. "Left or right?"

"Right."

"Would you like me to get a wheelchair?"

"I'm fine." And the sooner they got this over with, the better.

"Come this way, then." He turned and strode through a narrow hall, pushing open a door and waiting as she moved across the threshold.

Just one door. A sink. A small supply cabinet with two drawers. A chair. An exam table.

And a window that looked out into a tiny paved lot and the thick forest beyond. If she could get out the window and into the woods, she might have a chance at escape.

"King has a very good nose," Ian murmured, as if he'd sensed the direction of her thoughts. Maybe he'd just seen the direction of her gaze.

It was a warning, and she knew it wasn't an exaggeration. King had tracked her through the Florida swamp and followed her so closely it would have been impossible to escape.

Nothing is impossible.

The words whispered through her mind, a gentle reminder that she wasn't alone, that she didn't have to do this herself.

God would never leave or forsake her.

He wouldn't abandon her. Not the way Brent had.

Not the way her family had.

The last part was so much more difficult to think about than the first. So she wouldn't think about it. She'd just keep doing what she'd been doing since the day she'd seen her brother shoot a man: running, hiding, keeping herself alive.

There'd be time to think things through, accept the facts, work through her sorrow and anger after the trial.

She limped across the room, ignoring Ian's dark gaze as she sat on the exam table, pulled off her boot, rolled up her pant cuff and eyed the swollen blue-black flesh of her ankle.

The ankle looked bad, but Ian didn't think it would keep Esme from trying to escape. If she had an opportunity, she'd take it. He had no doubt about that. She'd glanced at the window at least a dozen times while the PA poked and prodded her ankle. She'd answered questions in a brusque tense manner that was at odds with her soft green eyes and delicate features.

She looked fragile.

He'd thought that the first time he'd seen her photo.

He figured a lot of people made the mistake of believing what they saw. There was no other way to explain her escape from witness protection. From the time she'd shown up at local law enforcement offices in Chicago, she'd looked weak and soft and a little tired. He'd seen the videotaped testimony. She'd been crying, tears streaming down her cheeks as she'd described what she'd witnessed. She'd been shocked. Scared. Horrified.

She didn't break laws. *She* didn't get into public altercations. No drinking, smoking weed, playing the odds. She conducted her business in a way that had built a positive reputation in the community. She worked with high-end socialite clients who paid a hefty sum for her organized and creative approach to wedding planning.

He'd read all about it online.

He'd wanted to know everything he could about Esme Dupree before he started playing bodyguard to her. He'd been certain he'd dig up some dirt, discover something that would convince him of what he already knew—she was as rotten as her brother and uncle.

He'd come up empty.

She didn't even have a traffic ticket on record.

Everything about her screamed "law-abiding rule-follower."

It was no surprise that her handlers in witness protection had forgotten what cloth she was cut from. They'd forgotten that she was a Dupree, that the same blood that ran through her brother's and uncle's veins ran through hers.

She might look fragile, but she wasn't.

She might pretend to be a follower, but she wrote her own playbook, and she followed her own moral compass.

Whatever that happened to be.

He hadn't quite figured it out.

He didn't really care to.

His goal, his purpose, was to get her to trial.

Justice and revenge. All in one fell swoop.

Except for one thing.

He did care.

It was the way he'd been raised. He might want to deny it, might want to turn away from it, might want to tell himself all kinds of stories about how Esme was just a Dupree and her problems were hers to solve...

But he'd looked in her eyes. He'd seen her tears. Now he was in an exam room with her, watching as her ankle was prodded and poked. She didn't complain, barely winced, but she looked done.

"We could x-ray this," the PA finally said, "to make sure it isn't broken, but I feel pretty confident that it's just a bad sprain."

"No X-ray," Esme said with a strained smile. "It feels better already."

She hopped off the table. Probably to prove the point.

"Just hand me an Ace bandage, and I'll be on my way," she continued, grabbing hold of the backpack that hung over Ian's arm.

King growled.

Ian hadn't been lying. King didn't like people touching his things.

And the pack?

It was currently his possession.

"You're probably going to want to stop grabbing things that I'm holding," he suggested wryly.

The PA had already stepped back, his gaze on King.

Esme didn't seem as worried about the dog.

She did release the pack, but she didn't back up. The ornery woman stood right where she was. Close enough that he could see dozens of freckles on her pale cheeks and the gold tips of her dark red eyelashes.

"I want to wash up and put on clean clothes before we leave." She tugged at the muddy fabric of her pants, her green eyes flashing with irritation.

"Okay." He handed her the pack, watching as her annoyance was replaced by surprise. She was easy to read. That would be helpful in the weeks to come.

"Just like that?"

"Sure."

"Why?" she asked, and he shrugged.

"Where are you going to go, Esme? Out the window?" He gestured toward it. "There are two marked police cars outside and probably five or six patrol officers surrounding the building."

She frowned but didn't respond.

"You wouldn't make it far before one of them spotted you. Even if you made it farther, you'd only be running from one danger into another. I think you're too smart to take that foolish of a risk." He glanced at the PA. "Can you bring that Ace bandage? My friend and I are anxious to get back on the road."

The PA scurried out of the room, nearly running down the hall. This was probably the most exciting thing that had happened in the clinic in years. He'd want to share every detail with as many colleagues as possible.

That was fine.

It didn't matter if Angus found out that his niece had been at the clinic. What he couldn't find out was where they'd be going next.

Ian glanced at his phone. No text from Max. Which meant he hadn't found a safe house yet. He was probably looking for one that wasn't in the FBI system. One that Jake wouldn't be familiar with.

"You know," Esme broke into his thoughts, "it would be a lot easier for me to get cleaned up and changed if you weren't standing in the room."

He met her eyes, trying to ignore the dark smudges beneath them, trying not to see the hollowness of her cheeks, the faded bruises on her neck that looked like fingerprints.

But he couldn't *not* see those things. She was a Dupree, but she was also a victim. His gut twisted at the thought. He'd gone into this kind of work to protect people like her, to prevent crimes, keep the bad guys off the streets and save other women from having to go through what Esme had. He couldn't look in her face and not realize how much she'd been through, how difficult it had been on her.

He turned away, closing the shades that covered the windows. "It would be a lot easier for me to do my job if I knew you were going to cooperate. I highly suggest that you do not attempt to leave this building, Esme."

He stepped into the hall before she could respond, closing the door with a soft snap that seemed to echo through the quiet building.

He stared at the closed door, trying to rid himself of the image of the bruises, the dark circles, the thin face and fragile body.

He didn't want to see Esme as anything other than what she was. He'd told himself that over and over again as he'd made the journey to Florida and begun his search. She was a Dupree. He wouldn't forget that. But she wasn't just a Dupree. She was a woman determined to do the right thing despite the danger. She was a person who'd given up her life to make sure her brother paid for his crimes.

She was a victim who needed someone in her corner.

Someone who would fight for her because she deserved it, not because of what he could get out of it.

Justice. Revenge. Closure.

They were what he wanted, what he'd been seeking for over a decade. He still wanted those things, but not at the expense of a woman who'd done nothing wrong, who—by all accounts—had done everything right.

King leaned against his leg, whining softly.

He didn't like the door separating him from the woman they were guarding.

But Ian needed the distance. Just for a few minutes. Because he didn't like the way he was feeling, didn't want the sense of responsibility that seemed to be settling on his shoulders.

Esme Dupree was an assignment.

She was the key witness in a federal trial, a fugitive on the run from a federal program. She was sister to the man who'd murdered Ian's parents.

But she had bruises on her neck and a price on her head, and that would change everything if he let it.

FIVE

She tried the window.

Because why wouldn't she?

It didn't open.

Ian had probably known it wouldn't.

Why else would he have left her alone with the pack?

Esme walked to the sink, turning on the water and splashing her face with ice-cold drops of it. She squirted soap into her hands and scrubbed her arms and her cheeks. Mud splattered the stainless steel and the counter, tiny brown blobs that slid along the smooth surfaces. She didn't bother wiping them away. Sure, she was tired, and her ankle hurt, but what she needed was a plan...and no matter how frantically her mind raced, she couldn't seem to formulate one.

She pulled black cargo pants and a light blue T-shirt from the pack. It was her only extra set of clothes, but it wasn't extra any longer. The set she'd been wearing was soaked through with mud and swamp muck. If Uncle Angus came hunting her, he'd smell the stench long before he spotted his prey.

Esme changed quickly, tossing the ruined clothes in the trash can, then she shoved her ID and money into one of her pant pockets. Her Bible was at the bottom of the pack—too big to fit in a pocket. She set it on the exam table. Beneath it was the photo of her family that she'd been carrying since she entered witness protection. Reginald, Violetta, Esme and their parents. Taken nearly twenty years ago, it was a reminder of what they'd once been—happy, connected, secure. A typical American family standing on a Florida beach that Esme couldn't remember. It was the only photo she had of the entire family, and she'd cherished it forever.

But now…

Now when she looked at it, all she could see was the sardonic gleam in her brother's eyes, the cocky way he held his head, the vast distance between Reginald and his parents. Esme and Violetta stood between them, arms wrapped around each other. Reginald stood a couple of feet away, slightly angled from the group.

She'd never noticed that. Not until after the murder.

She shuddered, dropping the photo onto the exam table and pulling her hair from the ponytail holder. The raw spot on the side of her head itched, and she ran a finger across the scabbed surface, telling herself she wasn't going to think about what had happened.

So, of course, she did.

She thought about the night Angus had found her, the swamp life teaming beyond the window. She thought about the quiet rustle of fabric and the horrible realization that she wasn't alone. She thought about trying to run. Thought about the way her uncle had grabbed her by the ponytail, yanking her back with so much force, a chunk of hair and skin had come out. She'd been blinded by the pain, terrified as he'd put his hands around her throat, looked straight into her eyes and tried to kill her.

If she hadn't been flailing, searching frantically for a weapon, if she hadn't felt the smooth domed surface of the heavy glass snow globe her mother had given her on the last birthday they'd spent together, she'd have died in the dingy rental near the swamp.

As it was, she'd smashed Angus in the nose with the snow globe. Blood had spurted out, and she'd run.

She was fast, but her uncle had almost been faster.

Because her hair—the long red hair that Brent loved so much, that Angus had used to stop her the first time—had caught in mangrove branches and nearly kept her from escaping.

Never cut it. Never dye it.

How many times had Brent said that?

"Not even if it's going to get me killed?" she muttered, walking to the supply cabinet and yanking open one of the drawers. Gauze. Bandages. Tape. She pulled open the other one and found suturing kits, alcohol wipes and scissors.

She didn't think through what she was doing.

One minute she had the scissors in her hand. The next, long strands of hair were falling to the floor. The scissors were dull, and she was tired, and the tears she'd been fighting for weeks kept trying to slide down her cheeks.

This wasn't the life she wanted.

This wasn't the way things were supposed to have worked out. She should be planning her wedding, not her escape from a federal officer, a crazy uncle, a corrupt brother.

"Everything okay in here?" Ian called.

"Fine," she responded, her voice catching on a sob. "Fine," she repeated, and this time she sounded almost normal.

Good. Because there was no way she was going to let him know how broken she was.

"You're sure?" he asked.

She didn't answer.

She was still cutting her hair. No mirror. No way of seeing just how badly she was butchering it. Just the scissors slicing through thick strands, the hushed rasp of that the only sound in the now silent room.

She couldn't escape out the window, but she could do this.

She'd learned her lesson. Ponytails were weapons that could easily be used against women.

"Esme? I'm coming in," Ian said, his voice soft and soothing.

Had she made some sort of noise? A quiet sob she hadn't heard?

She touched her cheek, certain it would be wet from tears, but it was dry and hot, strands of hair sticking to it. She wiped them away as the door opened.

She heard his footsteps on the tile floor, but he didn't say anything. Not until he was beside her, his muddy boots surrounded by dark red hair.

"Need some help?" he asked, taking the scissors from her hand. For some reason, she didn't try to stop him. She didn't protest or speak or tell him to leave the room.

She wanted to sit for a minute. Catch her breath. Try to stop the images that were filling her head. Blood and death, men she loved who'd proved to be nothing like what she'd thought they were.

Her uncle.

His hands on her throat.

"Breathe," Ian said quietly, the scissors snapping off one thick hank of hair after another.

She sucked in a lungful of air.

"There you go." He ran his fingers carefully through

her hair, cut off a few more strands. "Wish I were a hair stylist, Esme, but this is probably the best I can do."

She met his eyes, then saw the concern she hadn't been privy to before.

It surprised her.

She hadn't thought Ian had it in him to care. Not for someone with a name he seemed to despise from a family he obviously hated.

"He wouldn't have had the chance to strangle me if it hadn't been for the stupid ponytail," she explained. As if he'd asked. As if he really did care.

But, of course, she knew he didn't.

He was part of a well-oiled machine, all of it working toward one outcome, one result: shut down the Dupree crime family.

"Your uncle?" He set the scissors in the sink, his dark gaze never leaving her face. He was reading her. Easily.

"Yes."

"I'm sorry." He bit each word out. "Sorry we didn't do a better job of keeping you safe." His gaze dropped to her neck, probably to the bruises that still dotted it.

"I'm sorry my family's business is making money illegally. I'm sorry my brother has no moral values, no conscience and no regret. I'm sorry that my uncle is making your job more difficult. And I'm really, *really* sorry neither of them are who I wanted them to be."

"Or who you thought they were?" he asked.

"I wish I could say that. I wish I could say it and know that I had absolutely no suspicions, but I'm not a fool, and neither are you. My brother had a boatload of money to spend on whatever he wanted. I *was* suspicious and worried about where it was coming from." She released a quavering breath. "I admitted that during my interview with your people. It's why I hadn't spoken to Reginald in a few months and why I only had contact with him once or twice a year."

"You accepted a client who was deeply affiliated with him."

"I accepted a lot of clients who knew Reginald," she clarified. "If I turned every one of them away, I wouldn't have a business."

Of course, when she'd agreed to plan the Wilson-Arnold wedding, she hadn't known that Maverick Arnold was deep in her brother's pocket. She hadn't known that he'd gone to the police and sold some information about the way Reginald ran his business. She hadn't known that Maverick was a snitch or that Reginald had found out or that she was going to walk into the house Maverick and his fiancée shared and see her brother pointing a gun at her client.

Esme rubbed her arms, willing some warmth into her body.

"I see," Ian said, lifting the photo from the exam table and studying it.

"No," she responded, snatching the photo from his hand and tossing it into the trash. "You *don't*. You're living in your cloistered world of law enforcement, and you've been assigned the task of protecting a woman you despise—"

"I don't despise you."

"From a family," she continued as if he hadn't spoken, "you hate."

He didn't deny that.

She hadn't expected him to.

"All you're doing is your job." She nearly spat the words. "I'm living my life, and right now, it's not a very good one." She kicked the pile of hair, whirling away on her bad ankle and nearly toppling from the pain.

She limped to the door.

He'd left it open, and she walked into the hall, ignoring the surprised PA who was walking toward her, a thick roll of gauze in his hand.

He didn't try to stop her.

Maybe her new haircut made her look unstable.

She *felt* unstable, emotions roiling through her so violently she could barely breathe.

Ian didn't try to stop her, either.

But he was following. She could hear the click of King's claws on the tile floor.

She didn't turn around.

She had nothing left to say. Not one word.

The light went off as she reached the lobby, plunging the clinic into darkness. She stood where she was, velvety darkness pressing in, surprised voices calling out.

She knew where the exit was.

She could have crossed the lobby and walked outside, but lights didn't go off for no reason. Not in a place like this. There was no storm. No wind.

She stepped back, bumping into a solid wall of muscle.

Ian.

She knew it before she tried to move away, before his arm wrapped around her waist, holding her still.

"Wait," he whispered, the words ruffling her newly shorn hair and tickling her cheek.

"For what?" she whispered back.

Somewhere outside, an engine roared, and Ian yanked her back as lights splashed across the lobby windows and the world exploded into chaos.

Bricks. Sparkling glass. Dust. Lights. People shouting.

She was moving, dragged backward away from the front end of the truck that had plowed into the building.

"Move, move, move!" Ian was shouting, dragging

her into the still-dark hallway, the sound of gunshots following them.

And she finally understood. Finally got it. Finally realized that the driver of the truck hadn't just misjudged or made a mistake. He was there to finish what her uncle had started.

Suddenly, she didn't need to be prodded or pulled.

She ran, her ankle pain forgotten, her heartbreak gone. All the emotion she'd been feeling, everything that had been filling her up, replaced by cold hard terror and the driving need to survive and make sure her uncle and brother didn't have the opportunity to hurt anyone ever again.

Ian had been prepared for trouble, but he hadn't been expecting such a bold attempt on Esme's life.

He should have been, and he was angry with himself for the lack of foresight.

Reginald and Angus were desperate.

Desperate people did desperate things.

Including trying to kill someone in front of local law enforcement.

He scowled, his hand tight on Esme's wrist, his fingers digging into her smooth warm skin. He had to be hurting her, but she didn't complain. She was running through the hall beside him, her shoulder brushing against his arm.

Ian took a right turn at the end of the corridor, heading for the emergency exit that had been marked on a building map posted to the wall of the exam room. He'd noticed that, just like he'd noticed that the front of the clinic was comprised of large glass windows and a couple feet of bricks. Not a difficult facade to breach if someone really wanted to.

Yeah. He'd noticed. No extra points for that.

He and King worked protection more than anything else. They were good at it, but they generally worked with one or two other members of the team.

Right now, they were working alone, local law enforcement scrambling to contain the threat, but none of them specifically assigned to guard Esme.

He unhooked King's lead.

"Guard!" he ordered, and King growled, the sound deep and low. Not a warning. More of an acknowledgment that he was on duty and he knew it.

Good. The corridor was pitch-black. Even with his eyes adjusting to the darkness, Ian could barely see a foot in front of him. No generator cutting on to give some light to the situation. If there was a generator, the perp had taken that out, too.

They reached the emergency exit, nearly plowing into the door.

He felt Esme's arm move, knew she was reaching for the door handle.

"Wait," he cautioned.

"For what? The truck driver to come around the corner, guns blazing?"

"For me to open the door." He nudged her back until he knew she was against the wall. "Give me a minute to check things out."

"I'd rather—"

"Let's not waste time," he said, leaning in so close he could see her pale skin in the darkness, smell the fragrant soap on her skin. "The police probably already have the truck driver, but we don't know if he has friends."

She nodded. One quick, curt move of the head, and he turned back to the door, felt King pressing in close.

"Ready?" he asked, and the dog barked. "Let's go." He opened the door, and King sprinted out, racing across an empty lot that shimmered beneath a half-dozen streetlights.

Ian's cell phone buzzed. He ignored it.

His focus was on the dog.

He could see him running across the lot, heading toward a sparse stand of trees. He disappeared for a moment, the shadows swallowing him, then appeared again. Ian had trained other dogs, but none of them compared to King. The Belgian Mal was as smart and as driven as they came.

He waited for the dog to indicate. One quick sharp bark would be a warning that someone was nearby.

King was silent, loping from one area of the parking lot to the next until he was finally done and returning, tail waving jauntily in the artificial light.

"We're clear," Ian said, reaching for Esme's arm and pulling her closer.

"Are you sure?"

"He's my partner. We live by protecting each other's better interest. I trust him to keep me safe. He trusts me. You could probably learn a little from that."

"I learned plenty about trust from my family. I don't plan to ever forget the lessons they've taught me." She followed him outside, her hand on the back of his jacket, her fingers clutching the fabric as if she were afraid that he might abandon her like so many other people had.

He could have told her that he wouldn't.

But King was moving ahead, scruff raised, tail stiff. He sensed something.

Whatever it was, he didn't like it.

"This way," Ian said, tugging Esme into the deep

shadows near the corner of the building. Not wanting to alarm her more than she already was.

"What's wrong?" she whispered, and he knew she sensed it, too. The change in the air. The sudden charge of electricity.

King was off, running so fast he was just a blurry shadow in the streetlights as he headed back to the trees. To the darkness. To the shadows that could easily hide someone.

Ian pulled his gun, aiming in that direction. Not surprised to see the flash of light as a shot was fired. The bullet went wide, slamming into the back of the building a few feet from where Ian and Esme crouched.

A man shouted, then screamed.

No more shots. Just the vicious sound of King barking and growling.

A police cruiser raced around the side of the building, blocking Ian's view and his aim.

In any other circumstance, he would have run straight into the fray, gun drawn as he shouted for the perp to drop his weapon.

But these weren't other circumstances.

He had Esme to protect and no team members to guard her while he went after King.

The police officer jumped out of the cruiser, his gaze on the trees, his gun drawn.

"That your dog?" he said, his attention never wavering.

"Yes."

"FBI, right?"

"Right."

"You want to call him off or you want me to go in there?" the officer asked.

"The perp has a gun."

"I heard the shot."

"I'm not calling my dog off until I know he's disarmed."

"If I go in there and your dog attacks, I'm not going to have a choice as to how I react." The officer was issuing a warning, and Ian wasn't going to ignore it.

He shouted the command for King to return, praying the dog had managed to disarm the gunman. If not, there was a chance King would be shot as he ran away.

And Ian would have to live with that.

Live with the fact that he'd risked his partner's life for the sake of a woman whose family had destroyed his. The choice he'd just made only brought home the truth: he didn't want to protect any of the Duprees.

That was a fact.

It was also a fact that he'd walked into the exam room and seen Esme, scissors in hand, hair falling around her, and his heart had jerked with the kind of sympathy reserved for those who'd done absolutely nothing wrong but had still found themselves in untenable circumstances.

She deserved better than what she'd gotten.

That had been his first thought, his knee-jerk response.

She deserved better, and he could make sure she got it.

He *would* make sure she got it.

His first response, and maybe it was his second and third response, because he still felt it. Still wanted to turn back the clock and keep her from walking in on her brother's crime. Her only wrongdoing was having a name that made his blood boil. Her only mistake was in taking on clients that her brother sent her way. Those weren't things she should be punished for. They weren't things a rational man could hold against her, and he'd always considered himself rational.

Except when it came to the Duprees.

Maybe it was time for that to change.

He'd had more than one friend tell him he had to put aside his anger and move forward with his life. He'd told more than one of them to keep their opinions to themselves.

Not a very Christlike attitude.

His father would have told him that if he'd been around. He would have told him to let go of the need for revenge, to focus on justice and mercy and grace.

Ian didn't know if he could do that, but he could stop looking at Esme like she was the enemy. He could start viewing her as the victim she was. He could give her the protection she needed, offer her the support that was necessary when a person lost everyone they loved.

Could and would, because it was his job, because it was the right thing to do and because his father wouldn't have expected anything less from him.

He called King again, was relieved when he barked in response. Seconds later, King emerged from the trees, tail high, ears alert.

"What a relief," Esme said, and he could hear the sincerity in her voice, see it in her face.

He turned away, focusing on King, on the darkness, the trees, the chaos still playing out. For now, they were safe.

He planned to make sure they stayed that way.

SIX

King raced back across the parking lot, silent, focused.

He stopped at Ian's feet, sitting at attention, looking straight into his handler's face.

"Good job," Ian said, scratching him behind the ears, his focus on the police officer who was jogging across the lot.

The dog didn't look like he believed the praise.

His happy smile was gone. In its place was tension that even Esme could feel.

"You did do good," she assured him and then felt foolish.

She'd never been much of a dog person.

It wasn't that she didn't like dogs.

It was more that she didn't have time for the training and the walks and the attention they needed. Plus, her sister had a small yappy poodle who despised Esme. The feeling was mutual.

Esme hadn't wanted to add another thing into her already hectic schedule. Planning weddings for demanding clientele took all of her energy and focus. If she couldn't have a dog that she could make part of the family, she didn't want to have one at all.

So she didn't have a dog.

She didn't want a dog.

She sure didn't spend her free time talking to dogs.

King didn't seem like a typical dog, though.

He seemed completely in tune with Ian and absolutely devoted to doing his job. This time, his job had been to take down the shooter.

Was he disappointed that he hadn't been able to finish what he'd started?

"If so," she muttered, "I know exactly how you feel."

"What's that?" Ian asked, his dark gaze suddenly on her.

"I thought the dog might be disappointed. I was just telling him that I know how he feels."

"You were talking to King?" He smiled, a slow easy grin that softened the hard angles of his face and made him look almost approachable.

Almost.

"Is there a problem with that?" she responded. "Do you have a rule about people talking to your dog?"

"He's my partner, and you're welcome to say anything you want to him. He probably is disappointed. He likes to be in on the arrest."

"Instead, he's here babysitting me." She eyed the canine. He was staring toward the trees, his body still tense, his hackles up.

"And instead of being home planning summer weddings for rich clients, you're here," he murmured. "Is that why you're disappointed?"

"I'm disappointed that the people I love don't love me. I'm disappointed that the people I trusted couldn't be counted on."

"You're talking about your brother and uncle?"

"No." She was talking about her sister. She was talking about Brent.

She was talking about two people she'd actually believed in and counted on. The sad truth was she'd stopped counting on Reginald years ago. And she'd never counted on her uncle. Angus was her father's younger half brother. A product of a second marriage, he'd made just a few appearances in Esme's life when she was a kid. He'd been thirty years older than her, but he'd acted like a child—bullying others into doing what he wanted, whining when he didn't get his way.

She'd never liked him.

His criminal activity was no surprise to her at all, and she liked to tell herself that he'd led Reginald into a life of crime.

The reality, according to the FBI, was that Reginald had been running his *business* for several years before he'd asked Angus to join him. Her uncle had been more than eager to comply, but he wasn't the boss.

He most likely wasn't the one who'd called the hit on Esme. That was probably the hardest pill to swallow, and it was the one thing she couldn't bring herself to admit.

Especially not to someone like Ian.

"Your sister, then?" he guessed. "Or your fiancé?"

Both, but she wasn't going to admit that, either.

"Do you think the police officer has found the guy who shot at us?" she asked.

"Changing the subject?"

"Just getting back to a more interesting one."

He smiled again. A gentle smile this time. The kind of smile that seemed to say he understood just how hard this was for her. "There was more than one person shooting, Esme. The guy in the building, and the one in the trees."

"I know."

"So which one do you want to find out about?" He took her arm, and she didn't resist as he drew her around the side of the building.

"Either. Both."

"We'll go around front. I want to get you out of the open, so we'll check in with the officer in charge and then get out of here."

"And go where?" she asked.

"Wherever my boss sends us."

"The safe house?"

"Yes."

"Will it be as safe as my witness protection location?" she asked and regretted the flip question immediately. Ian had been trying to be kind. She knew that, and she shouldn't have repaid him with attitude.

"Safer," he said without rancor. No excuses. No explanations. He'd already told her about a leak in the agency, and he'd already told her the leak had been plugged.

"I'm sorry. That didn't come out the way I wanted it to."

"What way would have been better?" he asked, King trotting along in front of him, heading toward the front of the building and the emergency lights that flashed across the pavement there.

"Silence?"

He chuckled, his hand still on her arm, his biceps brushing her shoulder. "Silence is the better part of valor. Or so my father always said."

"He doesn't say it any longer?" she asked, even

though she knew she shouldn't. The question was too personal, and she didn't expect him to answer.

For a moment, she thought he wouldn't.

The muscles in his arm were tense and taut, his jaw tight.

"I shouldn't have asked that," she began, and he shook his head.

"It's okay. I gave you the opening. My dad has been gone for ten years. He and my mother were killed in a drive-by shooting."

Her heart seemed to stop, then start again, beating the slow unsteady rhythm of grief.

She felt like an idiot. Worse, she felt like an ogre.

She'd stood in the hospital room and accused him of being in his cloistered law enforcement world making judgments about her life. She'd been sure he couldn't understand the grief and anger she felt over her family's betrayal, couldn't understand the sorrow of her losses.

She'd been wrong.

"Ian," she said, his name just a whisper in the warm night air, "I'm so sorry. I know that can't help, but I am."

"They've been gone a long time, but I still think about them a lot. I'm sure you understand that. Your parents were killed in a small plane crash, right?"

"You've done your research," she said, trying to lighten her tone, take some of the sorrow out of it. Time did ease the sting of loss. It never healed it, though. She understood that just as much as she understood his pain.

"It makes the job easier."

They'd reached the front of the building. The once nearly empty parking lot was filled with emergency vehicles and teaming with first responders.

No more hushed summer night. It was loud and chaotic, the shattered glass and crumbling bricks spilling into the lobby, spotlights shining onto the wrecked furniture and huge Ram truck that sat in the center of the mess.

"Were you folks inside?" an EMT asked, his skin ruddy from the sun, his eyes wide behind thick glasses. He looked young. Maybe early twenties, his uniform crisp and new.

"Yes," Ian responded, his fingers still curved around Esme's arm. She could have pulled away easily, but she didn't. There was something comforting about his touch, about the warmth of his palm through her sleeve.

She wouldn't think about that too deeply.

She wouldn't question it.

She had too much going on, too many details to work out. Sure, she'd have to run eventually, but she still didn't know which direction or how far she'd need to travel to reach a bus or train station. She'd have to take one or the other.

An airplane was out of the question.

And she didn't have enough money left to buy a used car.

She couldn't hitchhike, and she sure couldn't walk. She'd be too exposed, too easy to find.

"Are you okay?" the EMT asked, his gaze shifting from Ian to Esme.

"Fine," she responded. "Is everyone else?"

"Aside from the driver of the truck, there were no injuries."

"Where is the driver?" Ian asked.

"I'm sorry, sir. I'm not at liberty to give out information about clients."

"I'm a federal officer. Special Agent Ian Slade."

He pulled out his wallet and flashed his ID. The EMT seemed satisfied.

"He's being triaged in one of the clinic exam rooms. He was shot in the chest. I'm not sure he's going to survive."

"Do you know who the lead officer is?" Ian hooked King back to his lead.

He let go of Esme's arm to do it, and she stepped away, putting a little space between them.

She didn't want to like him. She sure didn't want to rely on him. She'd made it a habit to avoid getting close to any of the police officers, federal agents or prosecuting attorneys. They were using her to get what they wanted, and she understood that. She also understood that she'd been cut off from everyone she knew and loved.

She'd lost everything, and she was vulnerable.

Esme had her faith, but having a friend would be nice, too.

It would be easy to cling to any of the men and women who'd been shepherding her through what had become the most difficult time in her life.

Easy and foolish, because she'd already had her heart broken once in the past six months. She didn't want to repeat that. She didn't want to feel that sense of surprise and betrayal.

Love wasn't supposed to be limited by circumstances. It was supposed to grow during the hard times. Not just romantic love. All love—family, friendship. Instead, she'd found that it had abandoned her.

She needed to keep reminding herself of the way it had felt to know the people she'd loved didn't love her in return. She needed to remind herself that she was a means to an end. Nothing more, and that if she let herself forget that, if she let herself believe she was forging relationships with these people, she'd end up hurt.

Sighing, she took another step back, scanning the parking lot while the EMT pointed out the officer in charge.

Maybe Ian would get so excited about interviewing the gunman that he'd forget he was supposed to be guarding her. Maybe he'd be distracted for just enough time for her to slip away.

There had to be a store in town. She could ask for directions to the nearest bus stop or train station. She might even be able to call a taxi to bring her there. If there was a pay phone or someone willing to let her borrow a cell.

That was the problem with going off the grid. It wasn't easy to get help when she needed it. There was no one to call, no knight in shining armor ready to charge to the rescue. Worse, there was no one to consult with, no one to help make decisions. Her failures were her own. Which wasn't a bad thing. Unless failure meant death.

She eyed Ian and King, both deeply focused on the EMT who'd pulled out a business card and was scribbling something on it.

She could try to leave now, and they might not notice. She told herself to do it. The federal government had already failed to provide the safety it had promised. She had no reason to believe that things would be different this time, that somehow the organization that had failed her would suddenly find a way to succeed.

She took another step back, distancing herself from Ian and whatever security he offered. The intuition that had kept her alive, that had sent her running from witness protection, that had woken her from sleep when her uncle had broken into her trailer, kicked in. She could feel it in the pit of her stomach, a warning. Not to hurry. Not to disappear. To stay.

She scanned the crowd, suddenly terrified that she'd see her uncle hidden among the gawkers who'd begun to gather. She didn't find him, but she knew that meant almost nothing.

She felt dizzy with fear, sick with the thought of catching a glimpse of him. Her head ached where the hair had been torn out, and she touched the spot, remembered how short she'd cut it. How short Ian had cut it. He'd been kinder than she'd expected, more gentle, and she had the sudden feeling that if she were going to be saved from her family, he would be the man to do it.

That thought kept her in place, frozen two feet away from the man and dog she'd been telling herself to escape.

"Good choice," Ian said, turning in her direction as the EMT walked off.

She didn't respond, because she wasn't sure it was. She only knew it had been the only choice she could make.

Deputy Sheriff Kennedy Sinclair didn't much care to have the federal government messing around in one of her cases. She made that very clear to Ian more than once while he tried to get information on the truck driver.

In return, Ian had made it very clear that the case wasn't hers, that the federal government was already neck deep in it and that he wasn't going to back off. No matter how much she wanted him to.

Three hours after the truck had plowed into the medical center lobby, they were still at an impasse, Ian sitting on an uncomfortable chair in the corner of an interview room that smelled like vomit and mold, listening while Deputy Sheriff Sinclair asked Esme dozens of questions about her uncle, her family and her enemies.

"Her enemies," he stated, impatient with the process and wanting to move things along, "are her uncle and her brother. She's told you that a dozen times."

"Thanks for your input, Agent Slade, but I'm aware of what she said." The deputy sheriff tapped a pen against the old table that she and Esme were sitting at and frowned. "And I'm sure that you're aware of how common it is for witnesses to change their stories."

"Not this witness," he said, and she scowled.

"*Every* witness. Ms. Dupree might think that she only has two enemies in the world, but that doesn't mean there aren't more."

"I'm sitting right here. I can hear every word you say about me, so how about you stop discussing this case as if I weren't around," Esme muttered, her hands splayed flat, palms down on the tabletop. Probably to keep from fiddling with her hair. She'd been worrying at the short strands, smoothing them down and then fluffing them up again.

Nervous energy. Twice she'd gotten up and tried to pace the small room. The fact that King was lying smack-dab in the middle of the tiny bit of open floor had made that nearly impossible. Both times, she'd walked to him, looked down at him, frowned and taken her seat again.

King had seemed to think it was a game.

He'd followed her to her seat, nudged her hand to get

the pet he thought he'd deserved and then retreated to the middle of the floor again. Currently, he was curled up, his nose tucked in neatly under his legs, his snout hidden, only his eyes visible. They were open. He was still on the job, after all.

"I'm sorry," the deputy sheriff said without a hint of remorse in her voice. "I'm just trying to get to the bottom of what happened tonight."

"I've explained everything I know. My uncle tried to kill me a few nights ago. He's probably responsible for what happened at the clinic, as well."

"Maybe." The deputy sheriff rested her elbows on the table and leaned toward Esme. Casual. Friendly. Ian had used the same interview technique more times than he cared to admit. "We found a jacket in the trees across from the clinic. Teeth marks in one sleeve. A little blood. I'm wondering if it could be your uncle's."

"I have no idea."

"You didn't see what he was wearing when he attacked you?"

"It was dark, I'd been woken from a sound sleep. Once I escaped him, I was too busy running for my life to pay much attention to what he wore," Esme said, a hint of irritation in her voice.

She'd planned to walk out of the hospital parking lot and run off again. He'd known it. He'd planned to give her the opportunity, and then he'd planned to stop her—a reminder to both of them that her agreement to testify against her family didn't mean they were on the same team. She'd stepped away. He'd been geared up to send King after her, and she'd stopped. Just…stopped. No limping run toward the trees or the gathering crowd, no trying to dart away and hide somewhere until he gave up the hunt.

He thought her decision to put her life in his hands had surprised her as much as it had surprised him.

She'd spent the past few hours avoiding his eyes. She looked scared and shell-shocked, as if everything she'd been through the past few months had suddenly caught up to her.

"Yes. I guess that's true." The deputy sheriff paused, tapping the pen more rapidly. "Can I be honest with you, Esme?"

"It's better than feeding me lies."

"This is a small town. We don't get a lot of crime here. I've called in the state police to help collect and process evidence. As it stands, we know who the truck belongs to, but we have no idea who was driving it."

"Did you fingerprint the perp?" Ian asked, and the deputy sheriff frowned.

"We're a small town and not well funded, but we're not inept."

"It was a question. Not a statement of your abilities." He kept his tone neutral, and she seemed to relax.

"I know. I apologize for getting a bit defensive. But the fact is that I'm a woman in a position that has been held by men for nearly a hundred years. Sometimes, I've got to act tougher than I am." She released a breath and got back to the matter at hand. "We fingerprinted the guy at the hospital, and we're running him through the system. So far, we've come up empty. We did locate a handgun near the jacket. We found several prints on it, and we're running those, too.".

"Any other evidence collected?"

"No, but I'm very familiar with the Dupree crime

family." Her gaze shifted to Esme. "We've had run-ins with some of their drug transporters during the past few years. Cocaine. Heroin. There's a little airport ten miles outside of town. They fly the drugs in disguised as commercial shipments and transport it through the Everglades channels and out into the black market. I'm certain I've only caught one out of every ten drug shipments. We search the cargo, but they're good at what they do, and they know how to hide their product." She sighed in obvious frustration. "I've been begging the town council to fund a K-9 program. We need drug-detecting dogs to really shut the runners down. So far, I haven't convinced them to fund it."

"I'm sorry my family is doing this," Esme said, her voice raspy.

"You have nothing to be sorry for. You aren't responsible for your brother or your uncle. I'm only telling you this because I want you to know that this isn't a good place to try to hide. Someone around here is on the Duprees' payroll. Probably more than one person. I'm sure it wasn't difficult for your uncle to find someone willing to come after you."

"Kill me, you mean." Esme pushed away from the table, the chair scraping loudly on the old linoleum floor.

"Yes. That is exactly what I mean."

"I need some air." Esme didn't ask permission. She didn't seem to care if it was safe to leave. She walked out of the room, her limp obvious. She'd never gotten the Ace bandage, and she hadn't had time to ice her ankle. Ian would make sure she did both. It wasn't much to offer her, but it was more than he would have wanted to give her twenty-four hours ago.

A Dupree but not like the rest of the family.

He still wasn't sure how he felt about that.

All he knew was that he couldn't keep viewing her through the lens of his anger and vindictiveness.

He followed her into the hall, King off-lead beside him.

He kept his distance as she made her way down a narrow hall and into a dimly lit stairwell. She jogged down the steps ahead of him, and he forced himself to keep quiet about her ankle, to not tell her to be careful.

She knew he was there.

He had no doubt about that.

But she didn't acknowledge him. She slammed open the stairwell door with both hands, her narrow shoulders shaking.

Was she crying?

He hoped not.

Ian had never been great at dealing with the softer emotions. He could handle anger, frustration and disgust with ease. He dealt with them a lot in his line of work. And he knew how to assuage fear, how to calm nerves.

But tears?

They were a different thing altogether.

Tears were vulnerability incarnate. They were hints at the soul of another human being, and he was never quite sure how to respond when he was faced with that.

A pat on the shoulder? A verbal platitude? A gentle hug?

They all felt awkward and foreign and fake.

Esme reached the exit and would have opened the door, but he touched her shoulder. Felt the fine tremors, the tension.

"You can't go out there alone," he said softly, and she whirled to face him, her short hair spiking out in a hundred different directions, her face still deathly pale.

"I don't want to do this anymore," she responded, her voice calm and quiet and reasonable. Completely at odds with the wildness in her eyes.

"Talk to the deputy sheriff?" he asked, knowing it was more than that. Knowing that she'd been pushed too hard and been through too much.

"Be here. In this place. With an uncle who wants to kill me. I don't want to keep running and hiding. I don't like danger. I don't like intrigue. I hate scary movies and books. I like weddings and happily-ever-afters and cakes with sugar flowers."

"I can get you some cake. I'm not sure about the sugar flowers," he offered, hoping for a smile, and felt a spark of gratitude surge through him when he saw the telltale curve of her lips, a subtle shifting of her energy.

She was calmer but not relaxed. "Thanks. Maybe I'll take you up on that. If I survive until the trial."

"You will, but I thought maybe you could use some cake now. When was the last time you ate?"

"I had a granola bar at noon."

"An empty stomach is hard on the psyche," he said, and she offered a real smile.

"You're afraid I'm going to have a mental breakdown."

"I'm afraid you're going to cry. I'm as opposed to tears as you are to scary movies."

She laughed a little at that, a hint of color returning to her cheeks. "You're going to be very happy to hear that I almost never cry."

"And when you do, there's always a really good reason?"

"Usually. Sometimes, I cry at weddings. When the bride and groom are the perfect complement to each other, when I've worked with them for a year or more and seen just how deeply in love they are. I get a little teary-eyed then, because it reminds me of my parents. They were great people. You know what I keep wondering?"

"What?"

"Where they went wrong. How two great people could produce a son who has absolutely no moral compunction, no conscience, no remorse."

"Your brother made his choices, Esme. They had nothing to do with your parents."

"What about Violetta's choices? She could have stepped forward and helped, but she's refused to say anything."

It was true, and he wasn't going to argue the point. Two people from one family had decided they were above the law. Three, if he counted Angus. He did. "You can't blame your parents for that, either."

"I want to blame someone. It's easier than believing that the siblings I loved weren't worth it."

"Love is always worth it," he said, and she smiled again.

"Maybe you're the one who should be in the wedding business, because I'm kind of done with the whole believing-in-the-fairy-tale-of-love thing." Her voice broke on the last word, and he was sure there were tears in her eyes.

"Esme—"

"Relax," she said, sniffing once and then turning

away. "I'm not crying. Just wondering how I ended up standing on the opposite side of the fence from the people who are supposed to love me."

She opened the door, and he motioned for King to move into place. The dog trotted outside beside Esme, ears alert, tail wagging. Warm, moist air blew in from the Everglades, bringing a hint of brine and rot. It was quiet here, the distant sound of highway traffic drifting on the still night air.

Esme didn't say another word. She seemed determined to leave, though, her limping stride carrying her across the parking lot to a cracked sidewalk that snaked through long grass.

"You know I can't let you go, right?" he said gently, and she shrugged, her hair glowing dark red in the streetlight.

"Esme," He tried again. "Don't make this more difficult for both of us."

"Sometimes, I get tired of following the rules, Ian. Especially when following them isn't doing me any good."

"It's doing you plenty of good."

"How so?" she countered. "I've nearly been killed more times than I care to remember. Maybe Violetta has a point. Maybe sitting on the fence and trying to stay neutral would be better than this."

Her words left him cold.

"You're not going to testify?" he asked, the question gruff and angry-sounding.

He needed to tone it down, rein in his own emotions. Esme clearly needed to talk this through. She didn't need him muddying the water with his less-than-positive opinion about her sister.

"Don't worry. I'll do what I said I would, and you'll

get what you want from me." All the warmth had left her voice, and that bothered him more than it probably should have.

"What I want is for you to live. That's not going to happen if your brother goes free." That was the truth. Or part of it.

"You're twisting the truth to make yourself feel better, Ian. You want me to testify because you want my brother in jail. He's committed crime after crime with impunity, and his organization is only getting bigger. Look at this." She waved at the darkness that surrounded them. "Reginald started in Chicago. In the past ten years, he's expanded to Florida."

"And nearly every other state in the country," he offered.

"Exactly. I can't let him continue, but there is a part of me that wishes I could. There's a tiny little piece of me that would love to do what Violetta is doing. She's not committed any crimes, but she hasn't betrayed her family, either. She has support from the authorities and from my brother and uncle. All I've got is myself."

"You also have me and my team."

"For a while." She reached the end of the sidewalk and stopped, turning her face up to the night sky. A million stars dotted the blackness, and he wondered if she noticed, or if she was too caught up in her pain and regret to see anything beyond herself.

"It's beautiful," she said, answering the question he hadn't asked.

"Yes. It is."

"That's the weird thing about life."

"What is?"

"It goes on. Even during the most horrible pain a person can imagine, the earth continues to revolve around the sun, the seasons continue to change. Flowers bloom and crops are harvested and people are born and others marry. God is still on His throne, and life goes on." She sighed. "I guess we need to go back."

"If you're ready."

"What else do I have to do?" She skirted past, King close by her side.

"Call your sister?" he suggested and instantly regretted it. He shouldn't be encouraging her to speak with someone who had a different agenda than the FBI. Esme was already struggling. Speaking with her sister might pull her farther down the path of regret and farther from the job they needed her to do.

"That would be nice, but I don't have a phone. Even if I did, your people told me that if I tried to contact anyone from my former life, I'd probably be dead within forty-eight hours. Cell phone signals can be traced."

"Not mine," he said, continuing to give her the option. Despite his misgivings, it seemed like the right thing to do. Not for the FBI or, even, for Ian. For Esme. She deserved to have a little bit of peace, and if talking to her sister gave her that, who was he to deny her the opportunity?

"You're offering me your phone?" She met his eyes, and he could see the suspicion in her gaze, the wariness. He couldn't blame her. For six months, she'd been a pawn in a game she didn't want to play, shuffled around by people who either wanted to kill her or wanted to use her.

The fact that he'd been part of that made him feel guiltier than he should have. Or, maybe, as guilty as he should be. If he hadn't been so caught up in trying to bring her family down, he'd have thought more about what she was going through—the terror and anxiety and loneliness she must be feeling—rather than what her name meant to him.

"Your uncle already knows you're in this area, but I don't want you to mention our exact location," he said, and it felt right. It felt good. It felt like he'd stopped letting his emotions, his need for revenge, cloud his judgment and started seeing the situation for what it really was. Not a chance to destroy the Duprees. A chance to keep the one bright light on its dark family tree from being snuffed out.

"So, you *are* saying that." She grabbed his arm, and he let her pull him to a stop. Found himself looking down into her face, gazing into her eyes. They were dark in the dim light, her lashes thick and straight.

She was a Dupree, but she was smart, driven, decent.

Beautiful.

It was a winning combination, and if they'd been anywhere else, in any other situation, he'd have told her that.

"Don't tell her what happened tonight," he said instead, letting his gaze drop to King. He was relaxed and alert. No sign of danger, and Ian was glad. Not just for himself and King, but for Esme. She needed a break from the chaos and drama, a chance to breathe in a little peace. "No mention of anything that has transpired since you and I met, okay? I'll give you fifteen minutes, and then the conversation ends. You agree with those terms, or it doesn't happen."

"I agree!" she said with more enthusiasm than he'd have had if he were calling a sister who didn't care whether he lived or died. Violetta didn't seem to when it came to Esme. She knew more about the workings of the crime family than she'd admitted. Her silence had kept Angus from going to jail.

He shoved the thought away, taking Esme's arm and leading her back to the building. "We'll do it inside. It's safer there."

She nodded, but he didn't think she heard.

She was smiling, nearly skipping with happiness as they made their way across the parking lot and back inside.

Weddings.

Happily-ever-afters.

Cakes with sugar flowers.

Right then, she seemed filled with all those things. And suddenly, he understood why she was so good at her job; he knew how she'd built a wedding planning business from nothing into a million-dollar company. Her energy was difficult to resist. Her joy and enthusiasm were contagious.

But her uncle was still on the loose.

She still had a price on her head.

And until the Dupree crime family had been dismantled, all the joy and enthusiasm in the world couldn't keep her safe.

SEVEN

Ian managed to find a small room where Esme could make the phone call. He also managed to convince the deputy sheriff to leave her alone there.

Well…

Not alone exactly.

Ian was sitting in a chair a few feet away, King lying near his feet.

Esme would have preferred they both leave, but she hadn't been able to convince Ian to let her have privacy.

His way or the highway.

That was the impression he'd given.

But he was letting her make the call.

That was all that mattered to her.

Her fingers shook as she punched Violetta's number into the phone. She felt nervous and uneasy, no point in denying it. Six months ago, she and her sister hadn't parted on good terms. Violetta had been convinced that Esme was going to destroy the family.

She'd been right.

But the family had been destroyed long before Esme realized what her brother was. Families couldn't be built and sustained on lies. They couldn't be nurtured when one or more of the members wasn't who he pretended to be. Esme had explained all of that to Violetta. She'd outlined her reasons for testifying against Reginald. She'd tried to convince her sister to cooperate with the police and FBI, to tell them anything she knew about their brother's crimes. But it had backfired.

Big-time.

Violetta had been livid.

So, yeah. They hadn't parted on good terms, but Esme still loved her sister. She longed to hear her voice, to know that she was doing okay, that the police and FBI hadn't come down too hard on her.

She punched in the last number and waited as the phone rang. Once. Twice. The third time, voice mail picked up, and all Esme's excitement and fear seeped away. She leaned against the wall, every bit of her energy suddenly gone. She left a quick message telling Violetta how much she loved her.

When she finished, she handed the phone back to Ian.

"Thanks," she managed to say, her eyes hot with tears she wasn't going to shed.

"I'm sorry she didn't pick up," he responded in a gruff voice, tucking his phone into his jacket pocket.

She caught a glimpse of his holster and gun, and she turned away from the reminder that he was there doing his job, that he only cared about keeping her safe so that she could testify.

Right at that very moment, Ian Slade was all she had, and he'd given her way more than she'd expected.

"It's not your fault," she said, walking to the door.

"You're giving up a little easily, Esme," he responded, and she turned to face him again.

"What?"

"You escaped witness protection and kept ahead of your uncle for months. I'm surprised that you're willing to make one phone call and call it quits."

"That was the agreement."

"We agreed on the terms of your talk with her." He pulled out the cell phone and handed it to her. "Give it another try. Who knows? She might be screening her calls. Maybe she's gotten tired of hearing from my team and the prosecuting attorney."

She met his eyes, realized that he was doing this for her. Nothing else. No hidden agenda. No desire for information or control. He wanted her to have what she wanted, and that felt…different. It felt nice. It felt like what she'd hoped to have with Brent but had never achieved. She'd loved him, and she'd been willing to concede on almost every issue. They'd almost never fought, because she hadn't found much worth fighting about. It seemed easier and better to let him have his way.

Her friends had said they were the perfect couple. They'd all wanted to be in a relationship just like the one Esme and Brent were in.

She wondered what they were saying now.

She dialed her sister's number again, her heart thumping with memories and with anxiety. She really did want to hear her voice.

"Esme?!" Violetta's voice rang in her ear, sharp and a little frantic.

"Yes."

"I'm so glad. When I realized I hadn't picked up when you'd called…" She paused, and Esme could picture her pacing her posh home office. "I couldn't believe it when I heard your message. I should have picked up, but the number wasn't one I was familiar with. And the police and FBI and press won't stop hassling me."

"I… Someone let me use his phone. I wanted to make sure you were okay."

"Me? I'm not the one in trouble. Are you okay? The FBI said that you weren't in protective custody anymore. I've been worried sick." She seemed to have calmed, her voice taking on its normal clipped tone. Violetta had money. Lots of it. She liked to live large. Big house. Expensive cars. Gorgeous clothes. Her persona reflected an upper-crust background that she didn't have.

Esme wasn't sure when Violetta had adopted it. Maybe after her first marriage. Her ex had been rich and snobby, his money buying him friends that his personality couldn't.

"I'm okay. Just…" She glanced at Ian.

He was watching her, his eyes oddly light in his handsome, tanned face.

"Just what?" Violetta demanded.

"Wishing I could come home." To her surprise, her voice broke on the words, some of the emotion she'd been trying hard to contain slipping out.

"You can. Just tell the feds you won't testify," Violetta responded.

"You know I can't do that."

"You won't do it, sis. There's a difference."

"Reginald killed a man," she said, the words making her feel sick and light-headed.

She'd seen it all.

The gun.

The blood.

The red stain spreading across the cracked linoleum floor.

"Sit," Ian whispered in her ear, moving her to the chair and urging her into it.

"Is someone there with you?" Violetta demanded, her voice shrill.

"I…"

Ian shook his head.

"No," she lied and despised herself for it.

"Look, hon, I love you. You know that, but you've got to back out of your deal. You can't testify against blood."

"That's not what Mom and Dad would say. You know they wouldn't. They'd say I should do the right thing, and that the right thing isn't always the easy one."

"Maybe so, but they're dead. You're not. I'd like you to stay that way."

"Then maybe you could do what I have. Testify. If you tell the authorities what you know about the Dupree criminal enterprise, then Uncle Angus will be tossed into prison where he belongs."

"Here's what I know," Violetta said, her tone hard-edged and angry. "You could die for the sake of a man you barely knew, a guy who was probably as big a criminal as you think our brother is. That man you saw shot? He had a record. You know that, right? Just because you think Reginald shot him, doesn't mean he was an innocent bystander."

"Think? I saw him!"

"If you insist on testifying, you could die for the sake of some idealized belief about right and wrong," Violetta continued as if Esme hadn't spoken.

"I could die because my sister won't do the right

thing." The truth slipped out. Stark and real and harsh, and she despised herself for it as much as she had for the lie.

"I would do anything for you, Esme," Violetta said, all the affection gone from her voice. She sounded like the person she'd been before she'd married into money and decided that having material possessions was more important than having relationships. "But both of us dying isn't a good solution to the problem. I love you, hon. I hope you know that."

She disconnected, the silence echoing hollowly in Esme's heart.

She wasn't sure how long she held the phone to her ear. Eventually, Ian took it, his fingers brushing against her cheek, warm and calloused and gentle.

She should have moved away, but she didn't. Not when he tucked the phone back in his pocket. Not when his hand cupped her chin. Not when he looked into her eyes.

"It's going to be okay," he said.

"You can't know that."

"Yeah, I can, because I'm going to make sure it is."

"Don't make promises you can't keep, Ian," she said, the words as hollow and empty as her heart felt.

"It's not a promise. It's a statement of fact."

"It's kind of sad that you're more determined to keep me safe than my sister is." Her voice broke, and to her horror, a single tear slipped down her cheek.

"Come here." He tugged her into his arms, and she went, because she needed his warmth so much more than she wanted to.

"All she has to do is tell the police what she knows

about Angus's involvement in the crimes my brother has been committing. If she did that, it would all be over."

"Some people have an easier time doing the right things than others do." He smoothed her hair, and she realized her head was resting against his chest, that she could hear the slow solid thump of his heart.

"Violetta is making a choice. Me or money. She's choosing money."

"Maybe, but your parents were right. Sometimes the right thing *is* the most difficult. Sometimes the easy path leads to the most dangerous places, and the most difficult road brings us home."

"I know."

"Obviously, Violetta doesn't. Not yet. So don't let her doubts shake your conviction." He said it kindly, his hand still smoothing her hair, the rhythmic thump of his heart soothing her soul.

It took a minute for the words to register, for her to realize what he was really saying: *Don't back out of your agreement. We need you to testify.*

The knowledge was like a bucket of ice water in the face. It woke her up, made her realize whose arms she was standing in. He wasn't any less biased than Violetta. He had just as much of an agenda, and she still wanted to stay in his arms, burrow closer, inhale the spicy scent of aftershave and soap.

She backed away. "You're afraid I won't testify," she accused. "Still. Even after I told you I wasn't going to change my mind."

"You're wrong," he said as she turned blindly and reached for the door handle. "I'm not afraid you won't do it. I'm afraid you'll spend the rest of your life regretting it."

"I won't," she bit out, her heart throbbing in her chest, her stomach churning.

"Are you saying you don't already feel like a traitor?"

"I'm saying that I know I'm doing the right thing. That's going to have to be enough."

"You didn't answer my question."

"Because I don't know what you want me to say," she responded, and she could hear the edge of sorrow and frustration and worry in her voice.

It surprised her.

She prided herself on her calm approach to life.

She'd won job after job because brides and grooms and their families had bragged about how easily she handled difficult situations.

She wasn't handling anything right now. She was just trying to get through this moment without completely breaking down.

Maybe Ian knew that.

He sighed, grabbing her hand and tugging her away from the door. "I wish you weren't in this situation, but you are, Esme. I wish I could give you some easy way out, but there isn't one. All I can do is offer whatever support you need and all the protection necessary to keep you safe."

"A personal bodyguard, huh?" she said, trying to smile but failing miserably.

"Call it whatever you want," Ian replied, brushing strands of hair from her temple and looking into her eyes, studying her face.

She wasn't sure what he was looking for, but he must have found it, because he smiled gently.

"It's going to be okay," he said, just like he had before, and then he stepped back, his hands dropping away.

"What now?" she asked, because she needed to say something, and because what she really wanted to do was step right back into his arms.

"We'd better get back to the interrogation room," he said. "The sooner we can convince the deputy sheriff to let us leave, the happier I'll be."

"Has your boss found a safe house yet?" She opened the door and walked straight into a tall muscular guy. She stepped back, nearly falling over in her haste.

He grabbed her arm to steady her, and she realized there was a dog beside him. Smaller than King, but watching her with the same kind of intelligence.

"I'm so sorry," she gasped.

"Don't be," the man said. "I never complain when a pretty woman bumps into me." He glanced past her, his smile broadening.

"I'm glad to see that they didn't toss you into jail, Ian," he said. "I was worried when Max said you were at the local police station."

"For once," Ian said, "I've stayed out of trouble. Esme, this is Zeke Morrow. He's a member of the Tactical K-9 Unit, and that's his K-9 partner, Cheetah."

"Nice to meet you." The words sounded stilted and awkward. Which was exactly how she felt. She'd been running from these men for months, hiding from the FBI and anyone affiliated with it, and now she was back in their custody.

She wasn't sure how she felt about that.

She only knew she was tired. No. Exhausted. There was an old vinyl chair sitting against the wall, and she dropped into it, her head swimming.

She closed her eyes for a second.

When she opened them, Ian was crouching in front

of her. "Are you okay?" he asked as King edged in between them and nudged her hand.

She scratched behind his ears and told herself she wasn't going to pass out from fatigue and hunger. "I'm fine."

"You're white as a sheet," he corrected, pressing his hand against her forehead.

"I'm a redhead," she muttered.

"I've never seen a redhead your particular shade of white," Zeke offered. "Maybe Ian was right. A little sugar might do you some good." He handed her a white paper bag.

"What is it?" she asked, her gaze shifting from him to Ian.

"Just something I thought you might enjoy after your hours-long interrogation. I asked Zeke to stop and pick it up before he drove here from the airport."

She peeked in the bag.

It contained a clear plastic container with what looked like cake inside.

She pulled it out.

Yes. *Cake.*

White with ivory icing and pretty yellow and pink flowers, and her heart hurt with the beauty of the gesture.

She met Ian's eyes again, and he was smiling, his face soft with what looked like affection, compassion and concern.

"It's cake," she murmured, as if it needed to be said.

"I told you I would get you some."

"Actually," Zeke interrupted, "I got it."

She heard him, but she was still looking in Ian's eyes, still seeing his smile.

She couldn't help herself, she smiled, too, some of her anxiety and fear seeping away. "Thank you."

"No problem. Like he mentioned, Zeke did all the work."

"Not just for the cake," she responded.

"No problem," he said again. "Now, how about you eat the cake while Zeke and I discuss how to get you out of here?"

He straightened, and she opened the container, found a plastic fork and a napkin in the bag. The first bite was sweet and light. Vanilla and sugar and flour and butter. If she'd had to put a name to the flavor, she'd say it tasted an awful lot like hope.

Things were looking up.

At least, as far as Ian was concerned they were.

Max had managed to find a safe house that was far enough away from town to throw Angus off their trail but close enough to be easily accessible. Zeke had arrived with Cheetah. Julianne Martinez was also on the way and planned to meet them at the safe house.

Three agents all devoted to getting Esme to the trial.

Yeah. Things were definitely looking up.

For him.

Esme didn't seem quite as happy, but she did have some color in her cheeks. The cake he'd asked Zeke to bring had done its job. The empty container was in her hand, empty but for a couple crumbs and a few smudges of frosting.

"Was it good?" he asked, and she patted her stomach, her hand shaking a little.

"It was the best cake I've had in months." She still sat in the old chair, her legs stretched out in front of her. Despite the food and the color in her cheeks, she looked exhausted.

"Good. Now, how about we get you out of here?"

"Deputy Sheriff Sinclair is okay with that?" she asked, glancing down the hall. Zeke was there, standing in front of a window, watching the parking lot as he and the deputy sheriff finished discussing plans for getting Esme outside safely.

Ian had left them to it, because he'd been worried about her. She'd been too quiet. For someone who'd been taking action and making decisions on her own for months, she didn't seem all that interested in the plans they'd been discussing while she ate cake.

That concerned him.

Months of fear and anxiety could wear a person down, make her feel hopeless and defeated. He didn't want that to happen to Esme.

"She said she has everything she needs from you. Come on. By the time we get to the safe house, there'll be a freshly made-up bed waiting for you." He took her hand, pulled her to her feet. She tossed the empty cake container and bag into a recycle bin and offered a shaky smile.

"That sounds great, because I think I'm crashing from my sugar high."

"Maybe you're just crashing from too many months of running," he replied, and her smile fell away.

"Don't, Ian."

"What?"

"Be so nice."

"I'm being me," he replied, leading her toward Zeke and the deputy sheriff.

"And making it really hard for me to not like you."

"Is there a reason why you don't want to?"

"Maybe I just don't want to be disappointed again."

"Again?"

"It's a long story. I don't have time to tell it."

"We're going to have plenty of time later," he replied, and she shrugged.

"You have something personal against my family, don't you?" she asked, the question so unexpected and sudden, it took a moment for it to register.

When it did, he stopped, turning so that they were face-to-face and he could look into her eyes. He wanted to see her expression while they talked, and he wanted her to see his.

Nothing hidden.

Nothing left out.

She deserved the truth, and he'd give it to her, if that was really what she was asking for. "Why do you ask?"

"I've been sitting there eating cake and thinking, and while I've been doing that, I've been remembering a couple of things you said about my family. Maybe not what you said, but how you said it. As if you despised everything we were."

"Not you," he corrected. "Them."

"See? Even with just those words, you sound angry."

"Do I?" he asked, but he knew he did. Just like he knew he was putting off the inevitable. They were about to spend a month in a safe house together. She deserved to know who he was, what he'd spent most of his adult life trying to do—take down her family.

"I'm too tired for games," she responded. "So how about you just tell me what happened?"

"I've known about your brother and his crimes for a long time. My father was a police officer in Chicago right around the time Reginald started making inroads into the crime world."

She frowned, and he could almost see her mind working, see her putting together bits of information and trying to connect them.

When she didn't speak, he continued. "My dad planned to shut Reginald down before he could gain more ground. He arrested quite a few low-level operatives, stopped several money-laundering schemes, intercepted a few drug shipments. Basically, he was making your brother's life very difficult."

He didn't continue.

He'd told the story to other people. He'd imagined telling it to one of the Duprees, standing in a courtroom somewhere and explaining the exact reason why he was going to make sure every crooked member of the family paid.

But he hadn't imagined this. Hadn't imagined looking in Esme's stricken face, seeing the knowledge in her eyes. She knew. He didn't have to tell her.

"Come on," he said, and he'd have walked away, but she grabbed his hand, her palm cold and dry.

"You said they were killed in a drive-by shooting," she murmured, her face so pale he thought she might fall over.

"They were."

"Are you sure it was him?" she asked, and he gave her credit for not denying it, for not insisting that her brother hadn't been responsible.

"Reginald showed up at the funeral. After everyone left, and I was standing by their caskets, praying that I'd wake up from the nightmare. I looked up, and he was there, standing a hundred feet away. He pointed his finger at me and pretended to shoot, and then he walked away."

"I'm so sorry, Ian," she whispered, tears slipping down her cheeks, the woman who'd said she rarely cried, swallowing back sobs as she stood in the stark white light of the police station. Her hair was deep red and spiked up around her head, her eyes deeply shadowed. He couldn't stop thinking about how she'd looked when he'd walked into the hospital room, seen her chopping off her hair because her uncle—her flesh and blood—had used her ponytail to keep her from running.

She must hate that, hate that she'd lost control in public, with Ian looking on.

She'd been through too much.

He'd made it worse.

If that was what wanting revenge led to, he didn't like it.

Didn't particularly like himself.

Let it go.

That was what his father would have said.

Let God deal with it.

He'd understood the truth behind that for a long time, but he'd never been able to make himself own it. He'd wanted revenge, and he'd wanted to be the one to dish it out. He'd wanted the Dupree family to suffer as much as he had. He'd wanted every last one of them to mourn and grieve and cry.

And then he'd met Esme.

She was as innocent as his parents had been.

He hadn't been able to protect them, but he could protect her. Maybe that was the key to peace. Maybe he'd come full circle, facing a choice about how he wanted to move forward in life. Maybe instead of taking two lives like Reginald had, he was supposed to save one. Save Esme.

Maybe.

"It's not your fault," he said, and for the first time since he'd been assigned this case, he knew that it was true.

"My family—"

"Isn't you." He wiped the tears from her cheeks.

"Ian—"

"You're tired. How about we discuss this when you're feeling more yourself?"

"Meaning not crying?" she asked wryly, swiping more tears from her cheeks. "You did say you were opposed to tears."

"On you," he responded, taking her hand and walking again, King trotting along beside them, "they look good."

She laughed, the sound husky and rough but still filled with warmth. "Better not say that, Ian. Next time, I might really let loose."

She was attempting to shove aside her grief and keep going with a good attitude. He'd never thought he could learn anything from a Dupree, but in the short time he'd known Esme, she'd taught him everything he needed to know about judging people on their own merit rather than on the merit of their family.

"You could let loose a floodgate of tears and you'd still look like the bravest woman I've ever met," he responded.

"I think that's the nicest thing anyone has ever said to me."

"Then I guess you haven't been around the right people," he responded.

She was silent for a moment, and then she smiled. Just a tiny little curve of the lips that made his pulse jump. "I guess running for my life has its perks."

"Like?"

"A bodyguard who knows how to say the right thing at exactly the right time."

"You two ready?" Zeke called, striding toward them, Cheetah at his side.

"I was ready an hour ago," Esme responded.

"Then let's head out."

She released Ian's hand and moved toward the door. He followed, more determined than ever to make sure she got to trial safely.

EIGHT

Esme didn't speak as she climbed into Zeke's over-size SUV. She didn't say a word as the two men got their dogs into the back. Zeke climbed in the front. Ian nudged Esme into the center of the bucket seat, grabbing her arm when she would have moved all the way to the other side of the vehicle.

"The middle is safest," he said.

She didn't respond.

She didn't have anything to say. She'd been fooling herself, believing in a fantasy, convinced that Reginald had committed only one murder.

One had been bad enough.

One had been horrible.

But he'd committed at least two more.

She had no reason to doubt Ian's story. She'd seen the truth in his eyes. She'd heard it in his voice. Apparently, Reginald had been killing people to get them out of his way for as long as he'd been running the *family business*.

How many lives had he taken?

And why was she telling herself that she was surprised, shocked, flabbergasted?

Reginald wanted his own sister dead.

He was working with Angus to make sure that happened.

Hadn't the FBI been telling her that for months? Hadn't they brought up his name every chance they got? It wasn't just Angus coming after her, it was Reginald. He was calling the shots and pulling the trigger.

"Are you all right?" Ian asked, his voice a soft rumble in the silent SUV.

"I will be."

"I shouldn't have told you about my parents."

"Of course you should have."

"It could have waited."

"Until when? Something like that festers the longer it sits." That was the truth. "Besides, I asked you. It's not like you just tossed the information out at me."

"It still could have waited. Seat belt," he said, and when she didn't reach to snap hers into place, he did it for her, his hand brushing against her abdomen, the warmth of his arm pressing against hers.

Comforting.

Just like his touch had been, his hug, his hands brushing tears from her cheeks.

Esme didn't want to think too much about that. About how much safer she felt when he was around, about how desperate she was to have someone she could count on.

She'd always been confident and had always known how to go after what she wanted. What she wanted right now was to be done with the trial and the testimony.

A month wasn't a long time.

She could do anything for a month.

Except maybe survive.

She shuddered, the warmth of the summer air drifting in the open driver's-side window doing nothing to chase away the chill that had settled deep in her bones.

"Here," Ian said, taking off his jacket and laying it over her, tucking the edges around her shoulders, his fingers brushing her collarbone and the side of her neck, lingering there. Soft and light and gentle.

That should have been all. Just a simple touch. His hand there and then gone. She met his eyes, felt something arc between them, the jolt of it making her pulse race.

"This is probably a bad idea," she said, and he smiled.

"What?"

"Whatever we're doing."

"Getting to know each other? We're going to be spending a lot of time together in the next month or so. Understanding a little about each other will make that easier."

"You're going to be staying at the safe house?" For some reason, that hadn't occurred to her. It probably should have. Ian had been talking about the safe house, about being her bodyguard and probably a bunch of other things that should have clued her in. Probably would have if she hadn't been so exhausted.

"What did you think was going to happen?"

"I guess I thought you were going to bring me there and leave."

"It would be difficult to be your bodyguard if I weren't close."

"Right."

"You don't sound happy about it."

"I don't really have an opinion." Except that he was the kind of temptation she didn't need in her life. That a few days with Ian could make her wonder what she'd ever seen in Brent.

Who was she kidding?

She'd spent a few hours with him and she was already wondering that.

"Sure you do," he said, and she frowned.

"Then my opinion is that my parents would roll over in their graves if they thought I was staying in a house with a guy like you."

"You think they'd take issue with me?"

"I think they'd have rather I stay in a house with a guy who looked like a toad, smelled like a troll and refused to shower regularly."

"No worries," he replied. "I won't be the only one there."

"And you couldn't have mentioned that before I went on my rant about trolls and toads?"

He chuckled, leaning back against the seat and giving her some breathing room.

She should have been happy about that.

Should have. Wasn't.

She liked having him close. He was a habit that could be easy to form and very, very difficult to break.

"You have the coordinates for the safe house?" Zeke asked as he pulled away from the police station and onto the road.

"Yeah. Hold on. I've also got another text from Max. He got a call from the local PD." Ian pulled out his phone and leaned over, speaking quietly to Zeke for several minutes. Esme heard a few words. Something about blood and DNA and a jacket. She could guess what they were discussing, and she could have joined in, but all she really wanted to do was close her eyes and sleep.

For the first time in weeks, she wasn't alone in the darkness listening to the sound of the Everglades, startling at every noise, pacing restlessly through the longest hours of the night. For the first time in weeks, she felt almost safe.

She closed her eyes, drifting into half sleep, the sound of a cell phone jerking her awake again. For a moment, she thought she was back in Chicago answering client phone calls and text messages. She opened her eyes, reaching for her purse and her phone.

No phone.

No purse.

Just Zeke driving the SUV, and Ian checking a text message, the blueish light from his phone deepening the hollows of his cheekbones, sharpening the angle of his chin.

Whatever he was reading, it wasn't making him happy.

"What's wrong?" she asked, and he tucked the phone away.

"Nothing you need to worry about."

"Which makes me worry more, so how about you just tell me?"

Rubbing the back of his neck, he let out a frustrated sigh. "Just a message from an anonymous friend."

"Another one?" Zeke asked. "Did Dylan forward it to you?"

"He forwarded it to the team. You should already have it."

"I really don't like being kept in the dark," Esme said.

"This has nothing to do with the trial," Ian reassured her.

"But it has something to do with my family, right?"

"In a roundabout way."

"Can you be any vaguer?" she asked.

"Probably. If I try hard enough."

"You might as well run the situation by her," Zeke interrupted. "Maybe she'll have some idea of who's sending the texts and why."

"What texts?" she asked.

Ian took out his phone, pulled up a text and handed it to her.

Word is that Mommy, Daddy and child have gone home.

She read it twice, trying to make sense of what she was seeing, attempting to put it in the context of the trouble she'd found herself in.

"Who are Mommy, Daddy and child?" she finally prompted.

"Daddy is the leak I mentioned. The one who gave away your location in witness protection. He's a rogue agent. He was working for your family." Ian frowned. "Your brother and uncle, I mean."

Esme narrowed her eyes, noticing the change in his rhetoric, the careful choice of words. She'd have thanked him for it, but she was reading the text again. This time out loud.

The words didn't make any more sense than they had before.

"Who are the child and the mother?"

"Penny and Kevin. His girlfriend and child. We think he's trying to get to his son. My suspicion is that he plans to take him and leave the country."

"What about the mother?"

"That's a good question," Zeke said, his voice tight and hard. "I wish I had an answer. The fact is, the agent is my brother, Jake Morrow. He's been on your brother's payroll for a while."

"I'm sorry, Zeke."

"Yeah. Me, too. If we could figure out who Anonymous is, we might be able to track Jake down, make sure he's stopped before he takes his son out of the country."

"We're sure it's someone who's familiar with your family and with Jake. Do you have any ideas, Esme?" Ian took the phone, tucked it back into his pocket.

"Me?" she sputtered. "I barely even know what you're talking about."

"We've been getting messages like this for months. Whoever is sending them seems to be trying to help us track down Jake. Unfortunately, the vague references aren't helping much."

"You think it's someone who works for my brother?" she asked, sifting through her memories, trying to find one that might be helpful.

There was nothing.

She hadn't spent much time with Reginald recently and the only vivid memory she had of him was his cold-eyed glare after he'd pulled the trigger.

"Probably," Zeke responded. "My brother was really good at making connections. He knows a lot of people. It's possible one of them is betraying him."

"I've never met your brother, so I have no idea if I've met someone who knows him."

"He went to a lot of your brother's functions. You might have seen him there."

"I didn't attend them." Not the extravagant Christmas parties, the over-the-top New Year's celebrations. Not even the birthday party he threw for himself every year.

She sent him a card.

She called him.

She made small talk about things that weren't important, but she never mingled with his crowd, because she'd never been comfortable in it. Violetta, on the other hand, had loved every bit of the lavish functions.

"But my sister…" She began, and then stopped herself.

"What about her?" Ian prodded.

"She might know something about Jake. She loved going to Reginald's parties. She enjoyed hanging out with his wealthy friends. I could ask her." Of course, that would mean calling again. It would mean having another dead-end conversation that would make her feel horrible. She'd do it, though, because she wanted to put an end to all of this. She wanted her uncle and Reginald in jail where they belonged, wanted peace for herself, justice for the man who died and for Ian's parents.

"Your sister has been less than cooperative," Ian said without a hint of judgment in his voice. He was trying hard to keep his opinion of her family under wraps, but his opinion was valid, his reasons justified. If she could help him, she would.

"She might be more willing to discuss things with me. We're family. That's important."

"It wouldn't hurt for her to try," Zeke said, glancing into the rearview mirror and frowning. "We may have a tail."

"Since when?" Ian shifted, angling his body so he could look out the back window.

Esme did the same. Not because she wanted to see danger coming for her, but because she wanted to be prepared for it.

Headlights.

Not close. Maybe six car lengths back.

"They pulled onto the road two miles ago," Zeke told him.

"And they've been hanging back all this time?"

"Yes. Pretty much the same distance."

"I'll call it in," Ian said. "See if we can get some local patrol cars out here. Turn off on the next road. I don't want whoever is in that car to have any idea of where we're going."

Where they were going seemed to be farther from civilization.

Esme hadn't been paying attention.

Now she was.

The town was behind them, pinpricks of light in the darkness. Ahead, there was nothing but an empty two-lane road. Thick marsh grass grew on either side of it. Farther away, a few trees jutted up toward the midnight sky.

No sign of any houses.

No business.

No golden arches spearing up from the landscape.

"If I can find a side road, I'll turn. Otherwise, we need to prepare for a rear attack. They seem to be picking up speed." Zeke accelerated, the SUV speeding around a curve, the headlights behind them disappearing briefly and reappearing again moments later.

"They're closing in," Ian said grimly as he pulled out his cell phone and dialed 911.

Esme didn't think calling the police was going to

do much good. The SUV was racing at a dangerous speed, and their pursuer was still closing the gap between them. She could see that as clearly as she could see the stars in the dark sky, the marsh grass sweeping sideways as the SUV passed.

"Hold on," Zeke said so calmly Esme wasn't prepared when he took a hard turn. She slammed into Ian, her shoulder pressing into his arm.

They bounced over a rut, and his arm slipped around her, holding her in place as the SUV hit another rut and another.

"Are they still behind us?" she asked, trying to free herself so that she could look.

He held her in place, his arm a steel band around her shoulders, his grip firm without being painful.

"Not yet," he responded, finally releasing her.

He had his gun in hand.

She hadn't realized that.

Hadn't realized how fast her heart was beating, how terrified she was. Not until she looked out the back window and saw the car. It was still on the main road but doing a U-turn, heading back the way it had come. Searching, she knew, for the turn.

"Looks like we're at a dead end." Zeke stopped the SUV and hopped out. No panic in his voice. No fear. He moved quickly and efficiently, grabbing a pack from the back, releasing the dogs.

Ian opened his door, letting the scent of briny water and decay fill the vehicle.

"Come on." He reached for her hand, tugging her out onto muddy earth. If they'd gone any farther, the SUV would be sinking. As it was, they were stuck. Going back would mean running straight into their pursuers. Going forward was impossible.

They'd have to walk out.

Run out.

Walking would do diddly-squat for any of them. She tracked the movement of the car as it crawled along. It wouldn't take long for the driver to find the road they'd taken. It would take even less time for him to find their SUV.

"We need to get out of here," she said, her voice too loud and tinged with a hint of desperation.

"We will." Ian snagged a pack from the back of the SUV, hooked a lead to King's collar and tossed his jacket into Esme's arms. "Put that on."

She didn't argue.

The faster she cooperated, the faster they could get moving.

That was how she saw things.

And she wanted to get moving, because she had a horrible feeling that Angus was in the car. Angus, the uncle who wanted her dead, who'd looked into her face and told her exactly why she had to die.

She shuddered, zipping up the jacket and following Ian as he headed through tall marsh grass, King on-heel beside him.

Zeke was a few feet ahead, his dog trotting nearly silently.

They weren't running, but they were moving fast, plowing through the grass and then on to drier land. She wasn't sure where they were heading. She didn't know if the men knew.

Wherever it was, it was away from that car and who-ever was driving it.

That was all she cared about.

That was all she needed to know.

She made the mistake of glancing back, of searching the darkness for the vehicle. And then she saw it, the headlights bobbing along as it sped toward the SUV.

She wanted to run. Wanted to sprint as far and as fast as she could. She probably would have, but Ian reached back and grabbed her hand, pulling her up next to him.

"Don't panic," he said in that same calm tone Zeke had used.

Did they go to school for that?

Did the FBI train them to keep their wits about them so that civilians didn't panic?

If so, it wasn't working on her.

"Why would I go and do something like that? Just because the car has almost reached the SUV and we're right out here in the open where any sniper can see us doesn't mean we should be worried," she retorted, the words spilling out in a rush of nervous energy.

"That's the spirit," he praised, not quickening his pace. Not glancing back. Not doing anything but moving forward.

Maybe that was a metaphor for life, but she wasn't in the mood to think about it.

Outwardly, she was staying calm, but inside?

Inside, she was a wild mass of hysteria.

Ian could hear sirens.

That was the good news.

The bad news was that their pursuers had already found the SUV. He didn't have to look to know it. He heard car doors slam. One. Then another.

At least two pursuers.

Probably armed.

Maybe with night vision goggles and long-range weapons.

That was more bad news, but it was also only speculation.

Angus had failed in his mission to kill Esme a couple of times. It was possible he wasn't nearly as well-versed in crime as his nephew.

He had found them, though. There was no doubt about that.

Ian wanted to know how.

He had a feeling it had something to do with Jake. The guy knew exactly how the Tactical K-9 Unit worked. He could have tapped into local databases and gotten a hit when Ian had checked Esme into the clinic. It would have been easy enough for him to pass that information on to Angus, and easier still for Angus to figure out that Esme would spend some time being interviewed by the local authorities.

After that, it was just a matter of waiting.

Anyone with enough money could hire people to do that.

Jake had the money.

That was what working both sides of the fence did for a person. It made him rich. It was possible it also made him foolish. If Jake were as smart as he liked to think he was, he'd have left the country when he'd disappeared months ago. At the time, the team had assumed he'd been abducted by Angus Dupree and that he would be used as a pawn to get Reginald out of jail.

It had taken months to uncover the truth. In that time, Jake could easily have found a way to disappear for good.

Instead, he'd stuck around, searching—it seemed—for his ex-girlfriend, Penny Potter, and their son.

As far as the team knew, Jake was still on the Dupree payroll. If that was the case, he could be hunting Esme. For all Ian knew, Jake was in the car that had been following them. If he were, he'd be a more challenging adversary than Angus. He knew exactly how the team worked, exactly how the dogs responded and reacted. He'd be able to anticipate and act accordingly. He'd know that they'd have abandoned the vehicle and would be hiking out with their dogs. He'd also know what weapons they had and how much firepower. What dogs they had with them and what each was trained for.

He'd probably assume that they'd be heading for the safe house. That was protocol. Get the civilian to safety as quickly as possible.

Jake would know all that because he'd done it. He'd lived it. But if Anonymous was correct, Ian's theory was wrong and Jake wasn't anywhere nearby. He was on his way home with his ex and their son.

That could mean Montana or something else, but it sure didn't seem to mean Florida.

He hoped.

Prayed.

They had enough on their plate. They didn't need to add Jake into the mix.

He glanced at his watch and adjusted their trajectory, making sure they were heading southeast. Toward the Everglades. The FBI had a house there. It hadn't been used in several years because it was too far from the nearest city. Most people didn't enjoy staying in such a remote location. Even if they were in hiding. At least that was what Max had said.

It was perfect for their purposes, though.

Ian wanted a place that was isolated. He wanted clear views and an easy escape route. Max had already arranged to have a small boat with an outboard motor delivered. If Jake or Angus managed to find them, they could escape into the Everglades.

First, though, they had to get to the house.

Up ahead, several trees jutted up from the soggy earth, their branches thick, their trunks broad. He moved between them, keeping Esme close. If there were snipers in the car, she was their target.

King growled, the sound filling the uneasy silence.

Danger. That was what the dog was trying to say.

Ian heard him loud and clear.

"Get down," he commanded, yanking Esme off her feet, covering her with his body. The first bullet hit the tree an inch from their heads.

She jerked, but he pressed her deeper into the earth as the second bullet struck, this time slamming into the ground, releasing bits of dirt and splatters of mud.

King was crouched beside them, and he growled again, his gaze on the area they'd just left.

"We're out of range for our handguns," Zeke whispered. "But I'm going to take a couple of shots and give you cover to move. There's a ravine straight ahead. They shouldn't be able to see you once you're in it. I'll circle around. Try to get a look at the perps. If the police show up, I'll deal with them."

He fired the first shot almost before he finished speaking, the loud report ringing through the night.

"Let's go," Ian said, rolling off Esme. "On your belly all the way. Keep the trees between you and the SUV. Don't stop until I tell you to."

"You mean between me and the gun?" she asked, sliding across the damp earth, her dark clothes blending in with the ground.

He followed, calling to King and smiling grimly as the dog pranced past. Zeke fired two more rounds, the sound masking what Ian thought was the sound of an engine firing up.

Were the perps on the run?

He didn't glance back to see.

He was focused instead on getting to the ravine and lowering himself into it, because Esme had disappeared somewhere up ahead, and he could only assume that was where she'd gone.

She might be out of sight of the gunmen, but she was also out of Ian's sight.

He didn't like that.

Not at all.

The ornery woman wanted to go it alone. She'd planned to hide until the trial. Without the protection of the team. She'd told him that. This had been the perfect opportunity for her to escape protective custody, and he'd handed it right to her.

He reached the edge of the ravine, lowering himself down and calling himself every kind of fool for letting Esme go ahead of him.

NINE

Esme's feet had hit the bottom of the marshy ravine, and she'd started running. Without thought. Without a plan. Just going as fast as she could toward some unknown destination, fleeing the gunshots, the car and, probably, Ian.

He'd been offering the protection she longed for, the security she craved. He'd given her comfort and smiles and, even, a laugh or two.

He'd been a port in the storm, a place to hunker down while the wind of Angus's wrath was raging around her.

But he wasn't a forever kind of thing.

He was a stopgap, a hero who'd run to the rescue when she'd needed him but who'd walk away when this was over and leave her exactly where she'd been when they'd met—alone.

Which was fine.

She liked solitude.

She enjoyed silence.

She didn't mind her own company.

And she certainly didn't want to be with someone just to fill a hole in her life.

Brent had taught her a lot about what she needed

and what she didn't. She hoped that she'd learned the lessons well.

Time would tell.

Time that wasn't filled with running for her life.

The marshy ground grew wetter, her feet splashing in a quarter inch of water. She needed to get out before she found herself in a creek or tributary up to her ankles or knees or shoulders. Wading through muck and dodging slithering, snapping, slimy reptiles.

She scrambled up the far side, feet digging into loose earth, hands grasping thick blades of grass. She was breathless when she reached the top, covered in dirt and mud. The sleeves of Ian's jacket hung past her fingertips, and she shoved them up, still moving fast. If she took off the jacket, she could leave it for King to find. That would let Ian know which direction she'd been headed, because she wasn't trying to outrun him or King or Zeke. She was trying to outrun the men who wanted her dead. If Ian and King found her, great. If not, maybe she'd find them.

For now, though, she was doing what she'd been told—running until Ian told her to stop. She shivered, her teeth chattering. Strange because the night was balmy and warm. She knew that. She could feel the sticky, humid air kissing her cheeks, could glimpse the clear sky and the moon resting just above the western horizon. The landscape was flat enough for her to see the distant flashing lights of emergency vehicles.

The police were on the way. It was possible they'd already reached the SUV and were rounding up whoever had been in the car. It was possible Uncle Angus was being arrested and that he'd be tossed in jail where he belonged.

Anything was possible, but she didn't think either of those things were likely. Angus had proved himself to be wily as a fox, moving mostly in the dead of the night, slipping in and then out without a sound.

Her uncle hired people to do the less subtle things— driving through clinic windows, shoot-outs in swamps. *He* liked darkness and enjoyed terrorizing people.

At least, that was the impression she'd gotten these past few months.

Her foot caught on a tangled web of marsh grass, and she went flying, landing hard on her hands and knees, her arms skidding in one direction, her legs in another.

She hit the ground with a thud, would have been up and running again, but a wet nose nudged her temple, warm dog breath fanning her cheek.

She looked into dark eyes, and then into King's grinning happy face.

His tongue lolled to the side, his eyes sparkling with what could only be joy. He'd found her, and he was very pleased with himself.

If she hadn't been lying flat on wet ground, the scent of decaying foliage in her nose, she might have smiled back.

"You don't have to look so pleased with yourself every single time. I'm not very difficult to find," she explained, but King had already darted away, heading back to his partner, tail high, carriage jaunty.

He was pleased with himself and ready to share the happy news of his discovery.

She could have gotten up and kept going, but she had as much hope of survival with Ian as she did on her own. More hope, because he had a gun. She had her mud-caked clothes and her will to live. Neither would stand much of a chance against a well-aimed bullet. Esme turned onto her back, staring up at the stars and the dark sky, her ankle throbbing dully. She didn't know what time it was…and she didn't care. In a few hours, the sun would rise, and she'd be facing another day of hide-and-seek. Winner took all. Loser lost everything. If Angus lost, he'd go to jail. If she lost, she'd die and her brother might go free. There'd be more crime, more drugs, more human trafficking and sorrow and terror and fear.

It was that simple and that awful. It was the reason she'd kept going for as long as she had. It was the reason she'd agreed to testify, and the reason why she wouldn't change her mind.

But right now, she really couldn't get up the gumption to care about any of it. She lay where she was, watching the night sky, thinking about how nice it would be if her life went back to normal, if she could simply close her eyes and open them and realize she'd been having some horrible dream.

The grass beside her rustled, and Ian was there, looming over her. She closed her eyes. Opened them again. Nothing had changed. Except that now he was crouched beside her. Not touching. Not talking. Just waiting, his eyes glittering in the darkness, King panting nearby.

"I wasn't trying to escape you," she explained. "I was just following orders. I guess running into the Everglades without any idea of where I was going wasn't the best idea I've ever had. I should have stopped at the bottom of the ravine and waited for you. I don't know why I didn't."

"Fear does funny things to people, Esme," he said, offering a hand and pulling her to her feet. "How's your ankle holding up?"

"It's fine," she said, ignoring the throbbing pain as she walked beside him.

"*Fine* is the word most people use when they think the other person doesn't really care. For the record—" he stopped and turned to face her, tugging his jacket tighter around her and zipping it "—I care."

"It hurts," she corrected. "But I can walk on it."

"You never got the Ace bandage."

"We were distracted by the truck that drove through the window."

"Right. It's been a busy night." He started walking again, his hand on her elbow as he helped her through the thick grass. She didn't mind that. Not at all.

"Once we get to the safe house," he said, his voice a quiet rumble on the balmy air, "I'm going to let you call your sister. You can ask her about Jake or not. I'm not going to put pressure on you either way."

"I'll ask her," she said, because it couldn't hurt, and it might help.

"Is there anyone else you'd like to talk with?"

"No one important enough to risk my life for."

"Not even your fiancé?" he asked.

"Are you fishing for information?"

"Not fishing. I'm out-and-out asking. According to your file, you're engaged."

"My file is wrong."

"Let me guess, he wasn't ready to marry you, but he didn't want to wait for you to be out of the program?"

"Something like that," she responded. "It's old news, though. I've been over it for a while."

"He was an idiot," he said, and she smiled.

"According to him, I was. He didn't want me to testify. He thought I was asking for trouble. He told me

Reginald and Angus were dangerous, and that he didn't want me to get hurt."

"Then he should have married you and entered witness protection with you to make certain you were safe."

"He's not much of a fighter."

"Not much of a man, if you ask me. As a matter of fact, if he was standing here, I'd call him a coward," he said bluntly.

"I guess he was, and he obviously didn't love me all that much. We had the whole wedding planned and paid for. I really thought he was going to be my forever. I was wrong."

"I'd like to say I'm sorry," he said softly. "But that would be a lie."

She could have asked him what he meant.

Should have, probably, but this thing between them? It seemed new and fragile and lovely, and she didn't want to ruin it by asking questions that would be answered in their own good time.

They'd reached a steeply sloping hill that led down to what looked like swamp—dark water snaking through thick foliage.

"Careful here. It's slippery," he said, his hand tightening fractionally as he helped her navigate the slick landscape. "You don't want to end up gator food. Fall into the swamp, and that could happen."

"Maybe we should head in another direction," she suggested nervously.

"If we do that, we'll never make it to the safe house."

"It's in the Glades?"

"Does that make you nervous?"

"I spent a few too many days alone there. I'm not all that excited about repeating the experience."

"You won't have to. I'll be there with two other team members and their dogs."

"Sounds cozy."

"It will be safe."

"That, too." Her foot slipped, and she'd have gone down if he hadn't dragged her back.

"Like I said," he murmured, "it's slippery."

"Any idea of how far we are from the safe house?"

"Too far to walk. One of my teammates is meeting us on the road about a mile from here. See that bridge?" He put his hands on her shoulders and turned her slightly, his forearm brushing her cheek as he pointed.

She'd probably have seen whatever he was pointing at if her heart hadn't been beating so fast, her pulse racing with something that had nothing to do with crocodiles or Uncle Angus or her near slide into the murky water and everything to do with Ian.

"She'll be right on the other side of it," he continued. "She'll pick us up there."

They'd reached the bottom of the hill, the pungent smell of the swamp filling her nose.

She could see lights in the distance, flashing rhythmically. Was it too much to hope that Angus had been in the car and that he'd been caught by the police?

"Maybe they caught Angus." She spoke the thought aloud, and he shook his head.

"Whoever was in the car drove away before the police arrived."

"You're well-informed."

He shrugged. "Zeke headed back to talk to Deputy Sheriff Sinclair and to retrieve the SUV. He sent a text before I caught up to you."

"You guys work fast."

"We've been doing this a long time," he replied. "That means we've got a system, protocol, things that we prepare for."

"If you're trying to make a point, you can just go ahead and spell it out for me."

"Once we get in my coworker's vehicle and head for the safe house, your days of calling the shots are going to have to be over."

"I told you, I wasn't trying to escape," she started to explain.

"That's not why I'm saying this. You've been in witness protection. Being in a safe house is different. You'll be housebound for most of the next month. If the trial date is extended, it'll be longer."

"I understand that."

"Good, and I hope you'll understand when I tell you that my team expects your complete obedience to the rules."

"The term *obedience* seems a little…archaic."

"It can seem like anything, but we're still going to expect it. Following the rules will keep you alive. Breaking them could get you killed. Before we get in the car and make the trip to the safe house, before the team and I agree to play bodyguard for the next month, we need to know that we have your complete cooperation."

"You do," she said and meant it.

"Really?" He raised a dark eyebrow, and she shrugged.

"Yes."

"That was a lot easier than I thought it would be."

"Dying young is cliché. I'd rather live awhile."

He smiled. "Good to know. Come on. We need to get moving."

He took her hand, and she didn't pull away.

She wanted this moment of quiet, of walking beside a man who seemed willing to risk everything for her. She'd think about what it meant later. She'd mull over his words, wonder about his answers, ask herself if she were reading something into nothing.

Later.

Right now, she was content to let things be what they were—walking hand in hand through the moonlit swamp, King prancing along beside them.

The moon had sunk even lower on the horizon, the swamp creatures slithering just out of sight. Nothing had changed. Her uncle still wanted her dead. Her brother was still a murderer. Her sister was angry, and her friends probably thought she was dead. Her business was being run by employees, and she didn't know what would be left of it when she returned.

There'd be no wedding, no marriage, no children, because Brent was exactly what Ian had said—a coward.

Yeah. Nothing had changed.

But some of what had stayed was good: God was still on His throne. The sun would eventually rise. Life would go on for as long as it did.

And she wasn't alone.

She had a team of people working to keep her safe. She had a dog prancing along beside her.

And she had Ian.

Somehow that made her feel better than anything had in a very long time.

It took longer to reach the road than Ian had anticipated, the wet spring and summer creating boggy terrain that made walking difficult.

An hour into the walk and Esme was visibly slowing, her limp more pronounced with each step. Julianne had already texted twice, asking for updates on their location and ETA.

She was clearly worried.

The safe house location couldn't be compromised, and sitting on the side of the road waiting for Ian and Esme to emerge was going to attract attention.

Or so she kept saying.

Ian knew she was right, but he couldn't push any harder than he was.

"So," Esme panted as she pulled her foot out of thick mud and managed another struggling step, "how much farther?"

"Not much."

"You said that a half hour ago."

He gave her an apologetic look. "I didn't realize how tough the terrain would be."

"It doesn't seem to be bothering King," she said. "Or you."

"We're used to hiking through stuff like this."

"This happens a lot?"

"No, but we run training exercises with the team. We don't make it easy. If you're going to be part of the tactical unit, you've got to be ready for just about anything."

"Sounds like wedding planning. But more dangerous," she joked, but her voice was flat and hollow, her fatigue obvious.

"Want to take a break?" he suggested. "My colleague can walk in and meet us here."

"What good would that do? I'd still have to walk out."

"Julianne is good at improvising," he told her. "We might be able to create a gurney of some—"

"No." She said it emphatically.

"You didn't let me finish."

"Because you were going to suggest that the two of you carry me out, and it's not going to happen."

"It's okay to admit when we're done in, Esme."

She shot him a glare. "It's also okay to admit when you aren't making a situation better, Ian," she responded, and he laughed.

He couldn't help himself.

Esme was different. Refreshing. Totally and uniquely herself.

"Well," she huffed, "it's true."

"I apologize. I was trying to give you options. Not annoy you."

"Everything is annoying me. The bugs, the mud, the horrible smell."

"Yeah. The swamp does have a unique odor."

"I was talking about me," she said, and he laughed again.

"I'm serious," she muttered. "I smell like bug spray and swamp mud with a hint of cake batter."

"More like vanilla and whipped cream," he responded, and she smiled.

"You're a funny guy, Ian, but we both know I've rolled in the muck one too many times today. I want a hot shower and clean clothes and a comfortable bed. I want to lie down and not have to worry that I'll open my eyes and see Angus."

"You'll have all of that soon."

"If I don't collapse from exhaustion first," she replied, limping along beside him. Despite her joking complaints, she'd had a good attitude about the long walk. She'd asked questions about King and about the training program they used for their working dogs. She'd asked how he'd gotten into police work and what his father would have thought about his work with the FBI. He'd answered because she'd seemed sincerely interested.

It felt oddly good to be with Esme. Despite the circumstances, despite her family name, despite all the things that should keep him from being attracted to her, he was.

"We really can take a break," he said, and she shot him a scathing look, but there was humor in her eyes.

"I think I explained my need for a hot shower and a comfortable bed. Taking a break isn't going to get me any of those things."

"It's possible King needs a break," he offered, and she snorted.

"King could probably walk for days and not get tired."

Hearing his name, the Malinois trotted closer, bumping Esme's hand with his nose the way he did when he wanted attention.

She scratched behind his ears. "You're a good dog, King. If I ever get my first puppy, I hope he turns out like you."

"You've never had a dog?"

"We traveled too much when I was a kid, and now that I'm an adult, life is busy. Brent and I were planning to get one, though. I do a lot of my work from home. I just needed a home with a fence and a yard. We planned to get that, too."

"There are plenty of dogs that do well in apartments, Esme. If you really want one, I can help you choose one after this is over."

"A few hours ago, I'd have said no. Brent was really the one who wanted the dog. I was mostly on the fence about it. My sister has a little yappy dog that hates my guts. I'm not so keen on it, either, so I figured I wasn't a dog person. Now that I've met King, I can see the appeal. They're good companions. If I'm going to be a lonely old maid, I might as well have some pets to spend time with."

"Old maid?"

"Cat lady?"

"I doubt you'll be either of those things."

"I'm certainly not going to be married. I already spent my wedding savings on the wedding that wasn't." She patted King again, and Ian could see her hand shaking. She didn't want to stop, and he wasn't going to force her to, but maybe he could distract her from the arduous walk.

"When this is over, I can help you choose a puppy."

"You're assuming we'll be living somewhere close to each other."

"There are planes, trains, automobiles."

"There are also a million dreams that never come true, and if I let myself think about getting through this, of coming out on the other side of it with a house and a business and a friend and a dog…" She shrugged.

"What's the worst that could happen if you believed that?"

"I might be really disappointed if it didn't happen. I've been through enough disappointment recently. I'm not up to facing another."

"I won't disappoint you, Esme," he said, the words pouring out before he could think them through. The promises right on the tip of his tongue.

Promises about being there for her, about helping her as she transitioned into whatever life she was going to create.

He might have said more.

He probably would have, but the soft hum of an engine broke the stillness.

Not a car or truck.

This sounded more like a bi-engine plane.

Which could mean nothing, or it could mean something.

Angus or his henchmen had driven away, but that didn't mean they'd given up.

He grabbed Esme's hand, pulling her with him as he sprinted toward the road.

TEN

She lost a boot and sock somewhere in the muck, but she made it to the road with one bare foot, a throbbing ankle and absolutely no breath in her lungs.

Esme would have stopped the minute her bare foot hit hard pavement. She would have stood for a couple of minutes, gasping and coughing and trying to catch her breath, but Ian was dragging her along as he sprinted up the road.

She knew what they were running from.

She could see the plane.

Worse, she could see its searchlight, aimed at the ground and highlighting the swamp and the marsh grass.

How far away was it?

A mile? Less?

They needed to reach shelter before it reached them. Otherwise…

She wasn't going to think about that.

Nope, instead she was just going to keep running, her hand in Ian's, King sticking so close to her side she knew that he sensed danger.

He barked. Once. High and quick, and then he shot forward, bounding over a small hill and disappearing.

Seconds later, he reappeared, another dog running beside him. A hound of some sort. She could hear it baying over the frantic slush of her pulse.

Her legs burned, her lungs ached, but she couldn't feel the pain in her ankle.

That was good.

What would be better was outrunning the plane.

It seemed to be heading toward them, swooping low over the marshy land they'd just left.

Were there footprints?

Was that what the spotlight was revealing?

"We're almost there," Ian said.

He wasn't even out of breath.

"Just so you know, when I get back home," she panted, "I'm going to train sprint runs. That way the next time a plane comes after me, I'll have a chance."

Her words were drowned out by the frantic baying and barking of the dogs, the drone of the airplane engines and the sound of a car motor.

Headlights flashed at the top of the hill.

There. Then gone.

Her imagination?

She wasn't sure, but Ian didn't seem concerned, he was heading straight for them, still running, still holding her hand.

The dogs met them halfway up the hill, the hound bounding excitedly, its vest glowing in the darkness.

A working dog.

A team member?

It had to be. Anything else would be too much of a coincidence.

Julianne's dog. That made sense, and so did the small SUV cresting the hill, idling there. No light, just gleaming paint in the fading moonlight.

It probably took only seconds to reach the car.

It felt like a lifetime, everything moving in slow motion. The plane. The dogs. Esme's legs.

The door opened as they approached, and a woman hopped out. Tall, muscular, quick.

Those were the impressions Esme had before the woman grabbed her arm, ushered her into the back of the vehicle.

The hound hopped in after her, scrambling for position as the door slammed shut.

And they were off. Pulling a quick U-turn and speeding down the other side of the hill.

Which would have been great.

Except that Ian wasn't with them. Neither was King.

"What's going on?" Esme demanded. Or tried to. Her voice rasped out, her lungs still heaving from the run.

"I'm taking you to the safe house," the woman responded.

"Where's Ian?"

"Throwing them off our tail."

"What does that mean?"

"It means that we don't want the airplane following us. Ian is going to make sure that if it's a search plane looking for you, whoever is flying it will think you're still running. At least—" she glanced in the rearview mirror and met Esme's eyes "—that's what I'm assuming the plan is. Ian and I didn't have much time to discuss it."

"More like you didn't have *any* time."

"True. He signaled me to take you and go. So I did.

I'm Julianne Martinez, by the way. Special agent, but I'm not big into titles. The dog is Thunder."

"He's cute."

"And loud?"

"That, too."

"I know! But it's useful when he's indicating. He's an evidence detection dog, and he likes to let us know when he's found something. He was very happy when he found you. He loves new friends."

Obviously, because he was nearly sitting in Esme's lap, looking at her expectantly.

"Usually, I crate him in the back," Julianne continued. "This is a rental, so I don't have that luxury. If he becomes a pest, just tell him no."

"Okay. Thanks," Esme responded by rote, but her mind wasn't on the conversation. It was on Ian, King and the plane. "They could have guns," she said, voicing the concern out loud. "They probably do."

"Ian can handle whatever they dish out. Don't worry about him."

"That's easier said than done," she muttered.

"Yeah. I know." She sounded like she did know. Like maybe there was a story hidden in the matter-of-fact reply.

She didn't give Esme a chance to ask for details.

"Do me a favor," she said. "Duck real low in the seat. We're going through a populated area. I don't want anyone to see you."

"Who'd be looking at this time of night?" she asked, but she did what she was told, pressing her chin to her knees, the scent of wet earth drifting up from her mud-coated feet.

One booted.

One bare.

She studied both, her back aching from the odd position.

She didn't straighten.

She'd told Ian that she'd cooperate, that she'd follow directions and do exactly what she was told. She'd meant it.

Esme desperately wanted to get through this alive, and she'd really like everyone else to get through it the same way.

"You doing okay back there?" Julianne called.

"Fine."

"Just a couple more minutes. This is kind of a shanty town, but there are definitely people around."

"And you think one of them is in my uncle's pocket?"

"I don't like to speculate, so how about I just tell you what I know? Your uncle and brother have been running drugs and people through the airport here for several years. They've made connections in the surrounding area, and they have several people on their payroll." She took a breath. "It wouldn't surprise me if Angus put out the word that you need to be found and stopped, and it wouldn't shock me if one of the people living in this little town was very happy and willing to make that happen."

"Nice."

"No. It's not. None of what my team deals with is nice, but that's why we do it. We want to stop people like your uncle from hurting and corrupting others."

"It's hard to be corrupted unless you want to be," Esme pointed out.

"Some people think that. I think that it's easy to fall into the wrong crowd when the wrong crowd is all you know. Angus and Reginald take advantage of that. They go after people who are already struggling, and they offer them a way out of poverty. Of course, the people who accept the offer don't realize they're selling themselves into modern slavery. They make money, but they're always beholden to the boss. If they try to break away, they die."

"It sounds like the Mafia," Esme said, sick at the thought of what her brother and uncle had created, disgusted by the image of an organization that fed off others, one that ate and ate but was never full.

"It *is* like the Mafia. I've heard a criminal profiler speculate that your brother was obsessed with the mob as a child, that he had a sense of helplessness brought on by your father's—"

"My father was a really great guy," she snapped and then was ashamed of herself for doing it.

None of this was Julianne's fault.

"I'm sorry," Julianne said. "I didn't mean to imply he wasn't. The profiler simply said that your father wasn't the kind of strong powerful man the Godfather represented and that your brother wanted to be what your dad was not."

"Or maybe," Esme said, the words tight and controlled, "Reginald was influenced by my uncle. Maybe he just wanted more than what he had. Maybe he didn't care who he hurt in his bid to get what he wanted."

"You're upset."

"This is my family we're talking about, Julianne. And I still can't believe they're such horrible people."

"The world isn't black-and-white. There are shades of gray. Your brother might be a murderer and a criminal, but he helped your sister a lot. That's something you can hold on to."

"He murdered a man in cold blood. He killed two people who'd done nothing wrong. He runs an organization that makes its money off criminal activities, and he doesn't care who he has to hurt to get what he wants." She blew out an angry breath. "That's pretty horrible, and it's pretty black-and-white. Should I not hold on to it?"

"What about your sister? She hasn't gotten involved in the business. She might not be cooperating with us, but she certainly isn't killing people for profit."

The words were supposed to be comforting.

Esme knew they were.

She knew Julianne was trying to offer encouragement, trying to make her feel better.

But there was nothing that could do that.

Saying Violetta wasn't horrible because she hadn't killed was like saying a boa constrictor wasn't deadly because it didn't inject venom into its victim. Snakes were snakes. And Violetta seemed to be one of them.

Esme shuddered, staring out the side window, Thunder lying on the seat beside her, his back pressed up against her thigh. She touched his warm fur, felt the soft rise and fall of his ribs as he breathed.

"You can sit up now," Julianne said quietly. Nothing else. She probably thought she'd crossed a line, but she'd only really spoken the truth.

Esme could have told her that. If she could have made the words form. Her brain knew what to say. It knew how to be gracious and kind. It knew how to put people at ease.

Right now, though, Esme could only sit mutely, staring out the window, watching as the darkness flew by.

Ian finally reached the safe house at dawn.

He'd hitched a ride with Zeke after he'd led the plane on a nice little joyride through marshy fields and swampland.

Eventually, the pilot had given up the chase. Either he'd realized that his quarry was really good at dodging the searchlight or he'd run out of fuel.

Either way, when he'd returned to the airport, the police had been waiting. They'd found an automatic rifle onboard. The pilot, a convicted felon who'd served ten years on drug charges, was arrested immediately. His passenger had an outstanding warrant, and he'd been taken into custody, as well.

Both were still being questioned.

Neither was talking.

That seemed to be the theme with the Dupree family's lackeys. They didn't talk. They were probably terrified of the consequences. A man who would murder family would murder anyone.

"This place looks interesting," Zeke said as he pulled the SUV under a double-wide carport. Julianne's rental was beside it.

The house did look interesting. Small. Purple. Standing on stilts that looked like a good hard wind would topple them.

"That's one word for it," Ian said, climbing out of the vehicle and stretching stiff muscles. He'd been going nonstop for days, and he was ready to crash. First, he needed to make sure that Esme was settled in and that the house was secure.

He opened the back hatch and released King, letting the dog explore the area as he did a circuit of the property.

Not much to see.

The front yard was mostly swamp scrub and mud. Beyond it, a small dock jutted into a deep green pool of everglade water. A canoe had been tied to a post, and he inspected it, checking for holes, life vests and supplies. Everything was where it needed to be, paddles sitting in the bow, life vests under the bench seats.

"How's it look?" a woman called, and he saw Julianne jog down stairs that led to the front door of the house.

"Good. Is this our emergency escape?"

"Yes. I'm hoping we don't need it, of course." She walked onto the deck, Thunder right behind her.

"Any trouble on the way here?"

"None. It was almost too easy."

"Meaning?"

"I don't know, Ian. I just don't feel comfortable here. The town we have to ride through to reach the property is probably owned by the Duprees. Someone there has probably noticed my bright shiny rental driving through. You think they aren't going to put two and two together?"

"Is there a reason why you think the Duprees own the town?"

"Crime. Drugs. Poverty. Do I need to say more?"

"I'll contact Max—"

"Already done. He's looking for another safe house while we speak. I want it somewhere less rural. We stick out like a sore thumb here."

Ian agreed. He didn't like the feel of the place any more than Julianne did.

"You guys having a party without me?" Zeke strode toward them, his dark eyes scanning the surroundings.

"No, but I'm thinking one of us better go inside and make sure Esme isn't planning another escape," Ian said, heading back across the dock.

"She's sleeping," Julianne informed him. "I made her shower, change and eat. She seemed upset when you didn't get in the SUV with us, and she was pacing around, asking me over and over again if I'd heard from you. I finally told her to take a nap. She did."

"You're sure?"

"As sure as I am about anything."

"You explained the rules to her when you arrived?"

"In detail. Shades closed. Windows locked. No walking outside without an escort. No phone calls, internet or contact with friends or family."

"Her response?"

"She didn't give me much of one. Just asked when I thought you'd be here."

There was a hint of something in the comment.

Curiosity maybe.

Ian made it a habit of keeping his private life private. He didn't enjoy sharing gossip about girlfriends or relationships, and he sure wasn't going to start sharing information now.

"I guess she'll be glad to know I've returned, but I'm not going to wake her. I'll shower, eat and get some shut-eye, too." He walked up wooden steps that led to a deck that wrapped around the house. King must have heard him. He bounded up the stairs, ears up, tail wagging.

To him, this was a new adventure. New place. New scents. New people.

To Ian, it was a nightmare.

Too much cover too close to the house.

Too many places Angus and his goons could hide.

He reached the front door and was about to open it when his cell phone rang. He glanced at it, frowning as he saw that the number was unlisted.

"Is that Max?" Zeke asked, stepping onto the deck behind him. "The sooner he finds us new digs, the happier I'll be."

"Me, too, but it's not him. The number isn't listed." He accepted the call, put the phone to his ear. "Hello?"

"Having fun in the swamp?" the caller said, the voice so familiar, Ian's heart jumped.

"Not as much fun as I'd be having if you were around, Jake."

Zeke stiffened, moving closer and leaning in to try to hear the conversation.

"You never liked me. Don't try to tell me that you did."

"I'm sure the feeling was mutual. Which is why I'm surprised that you're calling me and not your brother."

"Zeke needs to stay out of this. I don't want him hurt," Jake growled. "You have the woman. Esme Dupree."

"And?"

"Angus wants her."

"Sometimes we don't get what we want." He glanced at Zeke, nodding when the other agent took out his cell phone and started texting headquarters. Jake was probably using a prepaid cell phone, but it still might be possible to back-trace the signal. If Ian could keep him on long enough…

"He'd better get what he wants. If he doesn't, the team is going to pay for it."

"You think he can get close enough to any of us to make that happen?" Ian said, cold with rage at the threat.

"He might not be able to, but I can. I know exactly how you work. I know where everyone is, and I know how to get close enough to take you down one by one until you give me what I want."

"I thought it was what Angus wanted."

"He wants her. I want my kid to survive. You produce the Dupree woman, because if you don't, he's sending someone after my son, and I'll be sending someone after you and the team."

"I doubt you have anything to worry about. Angus doesn't want to make you that unhappy. You've done a lot for his family over the years," Ian said, stalling for more time. Julianne had joined them, her brow furrowed as she read the texts that were going back and forth between team members.

"I've cut my ties with the organization. I think you know that. Angus doesn't like that I've gone rogue, and he plans to find my kid before I do. He's got more manpower and more money, and if he manages it, he'll make me pay. Unless I produce Esme Dupree. The team has her, I want her. Hand her over by tomorrow night, or someone is going to get hurt." His voice was stone cold, and Ian had no doubt he meant every word he said.

"You have a location for delivery?"

"There's an abandoned church near the rental where she was hiding. Bring her there by midnight."

"That's too soon."

"Too soon for you to come up with a plan to keep her

safe, you mean? I'm not worried about that. I'm worried about my son. Midnight, Ian. I'm not playing around."

"You want to see your brother when we bring her? He's here. Part of the team protecting her."

Jake swore softly. Obviously, he hadn't realized his brother had been called in on protection detail.

"You come with the woman alone. If anyone else shows up, I'll kill her right in front of you. Understand?"

"You're saying you don't want to see Zeke?" Ian said, purposely prodding the bear.

"You don't seem to understand what's going on here," Jake said, every word clipped. "I don't want my brother hurt. I don't want you hurt. I don't want anyone on the team injured. I just want the woman."

"So she can be killed by her family?"

"So my son can live!" he roared.

That was it. He cut the connection, and Ian was left holding the silent phone to his ear.

"Did Dylan get it?" he asked, forcing a calmness into his voice that he didn't feel. The tech guru who worked with the team, Dylan O'Leary, was the go-to guy when it came to all things technical. If anyone could hack into a phone system and obtain GPS coordinates from a prepaid phone, he could.

As if in response, his phone buzzed, Dylan's number flashing across the screen.

He answered quickly. "Hello?"

"I got a quick trace for you. The cell signal on the prepaid you were communicating with was a hard capture, but I managed to find the signal tower that it was pinging from." As was his way, Dylan didn't waste time. "Looks like he's somewhere in Montana. Unfortunately, I can't give you anything more specific."

"Thanks, Dylan. That helps."

"Anything else you need?"

"Just an all-points to the team. Jake Morrow is on the move, and he's threatening to kill team members if we don't hand over Esme Dupree."

Dylan whistled softly. "He's crossing a line here."

"He crossed it a long time ago. If you're able to do anything else to pinpoint his location, let me know."

"I'll give it a shot."

Ian disconnected and met Zeke's eyes. "I'm sorry about this."

"Sorry about what? We're half brothers, remember? Jake and I barely know each other."

"For someone who doesn't know you, he seems really concerned about your well-being." He'd seemed worried about the team, too. In his own bizarre sociopathic way. "He doesn't want you anywhere near the church when I bring Esme there."

"As if we'd do that," Julianne scoffed, her dark eyes flashing.

"We wouldn't, but why not make him think we're complying?"

"I like the way you think," Zeke said. "Setting a trap for the guy who is trying to trap us. Jake is nowhere nearby, so Angus will probably show up at the drop place. We can take him down and end this."

"Let's run it by Max," Ian suggested. "See what he has to say. If he likes it, we'll move forward and come up with a plan."

"Anything is better than sitting around in this house, twiddling our thumbs and waiting for the boogeyman to come crawling out of the swamp." Julianne eyed the blackish water that stretched out behind the dock.

"I think you mean the swamp monster," Zeke suggested, opening the front door and waiting while Julianne walked through.

Both their dogs followed, rushing into the house without invitations. When they weren't working, they were family, and they knew it.

The team was family.

All of them connected and committed.

The thought of any one of the members being hurt because of the Duprees left a hard knot in Ian's stomach and soul-deep fury in his heart.

He wouldn't allow Jake to follow through on his threat.

Of course, there was only one way to stop him: stop Angus Dupree and shut down the Dupree crime family forever.

ELEVEN

Julianne and Zeke left the safe house at 9:45 p.m.

Esme didn't know exactly what they were doing, but she was certain it had something to do with her. Julianne had compared their height, commented that she'd pass for Esme only if Angus was blind and stupid, then strapped on a gun, pulled on a jacket and strode out the door.

That had been three hours ago.

They still hadn't returned, and Ian was pacing the little house like a caged animal, moving back and forth across the living room, checking his cell phone, doing everything but walking outside and shouting for God to give him some answers.

"I'm sure they'll contact you as soon as they finish doing whatever it is they're doing," she finally said, and he turned to face her.

He'd showered and changed, shaved and napped.

She knew all those things because Julianne had seemed determined to keep Esme informed of everything except her plans for the night. She also knew that he was angry. She could see it in the tautness of his muscles, the tightness of his jaw.

"This is about my uncle, isn't it? He's causing more trouble."

"Your uncle wants us to turn you over to him tonight. If we don't, there's been threats made against team members."

"What kind of threats?"

"The normal, everyday someone-is-going-to-die threats," he gritted out, crossing the room and sitting down beside her.

She'd chosen the couch. It was the only piece of furniture in the room that wasn't covered in psychedelic fabric. The armchair was lime green and bright pink stripes. The love seat was robin egg blue with huge yellow and purple flowers.

The sofa was a muted ivory that was surprisingly clean and soft. She'd sat there because it had reminded her of her old life—of weddings and brides and dresses.

She wasn't sure why Ian chose it. There were plenty of other places to sit. She liked him there, though. She wasn't going to lie. It felt good to have his warm arm pressed against her shoulder. It felt good to not be alone.

He lifted her hand, frowning at the scratches that marred her palm. "I didn't realize you'd gotten hurt when you fell last night."

He traced a line from her palm to her wrist, his fingers warm on her cool skin. Heat shot through her, and she almost pulled away, but this was Ian, and being near him felt like being home—so right, so wonderful that she couldn't imagine ever wanting to be anywhere else.

"I got hurt when I realized what my family was. I didn't even feel the scratches," she admitted.

He studied her face. Not speaking for such a long time, she was tempted to fill the silence, to beg forgiveness for all the trouble her family had caused, all the people who had been hurt because of them.

"When I took this assignment," he finally said, "I wasn't expecting to like you."

"I got that impression," she admitted, and he smiled.

"Yeah, I know. I'm sorry about that. I'm also sorry that we didn't apprehend Angus before he got to you." He touched the side of her neck, sliding his finger along what she knew were the fading bruises her uncle had left. She resisted the urge to lean closer, to let her fingers slide into his hair.

"It's not anyone's fault. He's got a lot of money, and he likes to hire people to do his dirty work."

"I'm hoping he's planning to do his own work tonight."

"You think he'll show up?"

"I don't know. Julianne and Zeke are prepared for it. We went over all the variables."

"Are you upset because you had to stay here and guard me?" she asked softly.

"I'm upset that you have to go through this. I'm upset that Jake Morrow and Angus Dupree are wandering free while we hide in this house. I'm not upset about guarding you. I told you before, Esme, I'll keep doing it as long as it's necessary."

"Don't say that. It might be necessary forever," she cautioned with a laugh that sounded a little too loud and a little too phony.

"That's an interesting thought," he responded. "How about we revisit it after this is over?"

"You're kidding, right?"

"Why would I be?"

"Because I'm a Dupree and you're trying to bring

down my entire family?" she said, her mouth dry with something that felt a lot like nerves.

"I'm going after criminals, Esme. You're not one of them. I'm not going to lie. That wasn't my mind-set when we met. You were the last assignment I wanted to take. My boss had other plans." He shrugged. "Or, maybe, God did."

"Probably God did," she said, and he smiled.

"My father would agree."

"You don't?"

"If you'd asked me a week ago, I'd have said I didn't know. It's tough to see God in things that make us unhappy. Now…" He shook his head. "I can't deny that I see Him working. Getting to know you has mended something in me that I didn't know was broken. Revenge tastes sweet when you're first going after it, but it turns bitter in the end. I'm glad God didn't let me get that far down the path."

"My uncle and brother need to pay for what they did."

"They do. But there's a difference between revenge and justice. Spending time with you has clarified that for me." He brushed a few strands of hair from her forehead, cocking his head to the side, studying her again.

"You cleaned up your haircut, didn't you?" he finally asked.

"Julianne helped me."

"She did a good job. Next time, I'll drive you to the hairdressers instead of helping you with the scissors."

"You're planning a lot of things for a future we may not have."

"We're going to have a future, and I have a feeling we're going to be spending a lot of it together." He ran his knuckles down her cheek, looked so deeply into her eyes, she thought he might be seeing her soul.

Her hand moved of its own accord, her palm sliding along the warm column of his neck, her fingers smoothing the silky strands of his hair.

He didn't pull back, didn't tell her to stop, didn't list a dozen reasons why it wasn't appropriate for them to be sitting the way they were. He just looked into her eyes and into her heart, and she looked into his, seeing things that she hadn't expected. Attraction. Interest. Compassion.

His cell phone buzzed, and she jerked back, the sound like a splash of ice water in her face.

He glanced down at his phone screen, frowning as he read the text.

"What's wrong?"

"Things didn't go down the way we'd hoped. Angus sent three men to the church. There was a shoot-out. All three are dead."

"What about Zeke and Julianne?"

"Zeke was hit. Doesn't sound like a serious injury, but Julianne is accompanying him to the hospital."

"And Angus is still on the loose." She said what they were both thinking, named the thing neither of them wanted.

"Right." He bit out the answer, his eyes flashing with banked fury.

She wanted to offer words of comfort. She wanted to tell him that Angus would be caught. She wanted to say that justice would be served, and that God would bring them all through this safely.

She wanted to say a dozen things that she hoped would be true, but he was moving across the room, dialing a number, talking to someone, each word a hard staccato beat.

King walked next to him, whining softly in response

to the wild energy that suddenly seemed to fill the room, and Esme was redundant—an extra in a drama she should have had no part in.

She stood, limping across the living room and down a narrow hall. Her room was at the end, a single door that opened into a plum-colored boxy space. The bed sat in the middle, a peacock blue comforter clashing with the walls. She turned off the light, let the darkness hide the garish decor.

She could still hear Ian, his voice drifting through the closed door. She thought she heard him talking about a new plan. One that involved Jake Morrow.

She didn't leave the room and ask him to clarify.

He was busy. Doing what he was paid to do. Protecting civilians from criminals like Angus.

She shuddered, pulling the pillow over her eyes, pressing it hard against lids that seemed to want to let tears seep out. She prayed for Zeke, that his injury really was minor and that he'd recover quickly. For Ian, Julianne and the rest of the team.

And then she prayed for her family. Prayed that Violetta would do the right thing, and that Angus and Reginald would pay for their crimes.

When she finished, she lay still, the house settling around her, Ian's voice silent, the only sound the soft lap of wind against the windows and the rhythmic click of King's claws as he walked from room to room, waiting for danger that Esme hoped would never come.

Zeke and Julianne arrived at the house an hour before dawn.

Neither of them looked happy.

Ian wasn't happy, either. The thick bandage that

peeked out from under the short sleeve of Zeke's shirt was a stark reminder of just how bad the mission had gone.

Three gunmen dead. One federal officer injured.

And no sign of Angus.

He was out there, though.

Haunting the streets, waiting for news and for an opportunity to strike again.

"How's the shoulder?" Ian asked as Zeke dropped into the gaudy recliner.

"It would be better if I didn't have a bullet hole in it."

"Don't exaggerate," Julianne chided. "It barely grazed you."

"Tell that to my shoulder. Maybe it will stop throbbing."

"They offered you pain meds," she chided.

"I'm on duty."

"I can call Max and ask him to send someone else," Ian offered, and Zeke scowled.

"Don't even think about it. This—" he poked at the bandage "—has made things a lot more personal."

"Did we get an ID on any of the gunmen?" Ian asked.

"Locals," Julianne replied. "The deputy sheriff knew all three by sight."

"I guess you were right about the Duprees owning this town." Zeke stood and walked into the kitchen, opening the fridge and surveying its contents. "Eggs, anyone?"

"Are you cooking?" Ian asked.

"Only if I have to. The arm is a little sore."

"I'll take care of it." Ian needed to do something. Beating eggs seemed a whole lot less violent than beating Angus to a bloody pulp.

He frowned as he poured the eggs into a hot pan.

Justice. Not revenge.

But it was hard to keep that in mind when a guy like Angus was out there.

His cell buzzed, and he pulled it out, glancing at the text as he spooned cooked eggs onto plates. It was from Dylan, the message making Ian's pulse race.

Max has been injured. Shot while he was walking his dog. Should be fine. He'll call once he's been triaged.

Julianne and Zeke must have received the same text.

They were moving toward him, phones in hand, looks of shock and outrage on their faces.

"Jake," Ian said. Just that. They knew. He knew.

No one else could have done this. No one else would have.

"I thought maybe he was yanking our chains, trying to get his way, but he really did mean he was going to pick us off one by one if we didn't hand Esme over." Zeke sounded as furious as Ian felt.

"He acted quickly. Didn't even wait a few hours. He must have gotten a call from Angus and gone after the closest team member," Ian said.

"Which means he's hanging out somewhere close to headquarters." Julianne frowned. "He's brazen."

"He's a fool," Ian corrected darkly. "He thinks he's too smart and too fast to be caught."

"So far, he's been right." Zeke smoothed down the edge of his bandage and grabbed a plate of eggs. He shoveled in a mouthful as he eyed the message.

"He's been right because he's been lying low. Now that he's showing himself more, we should be able to catch him," Ian responded.

"Catch him. Catch Angus. Go back to our regularly scheduled program," Julianne agreed.

Ian's phone rang. He glanced at the number.

Unlisted.

Again.

And he knew exactly who it was.

He answered, every bit of the rage he felt seeping into his voice. "What do you want, Jake?"

"Esme Dupree. I told you that. Apparently, you weren't listening."

"I listened. Now it's your turn. You're going down for this, Morrow. I'm going to make certain of it."

"You'll have to find me first, and that's proved really difficult for you and the team. So how about we call a truce? You promise me the woman, and I stop shooting at team members."

"How about you jump off the nearest—"

Julianne snatched the phone from his hand, putting it on speakerphone.

"Jake?" she said, her voice a lot calmer than Ian's had been. "It's Julianne. I think you know the team never makes deals with criminals. Back off and give us space to do our job. We'll protect your son, if you don't get in our way."

"Like you protected Max?" he said with a snide laugh that made Ian's blood run cold.

"I was shot tonight, bro," Zeke said angrily. "Going after the goons your friend hired. How do you feel about that?"

"I told you to stay away. I warned you. Angus doesn't care who he kills."

"It doesn't seem like you do, either," Ian pointed out.

"You're wrong. I have to make tough choices. I got

in deeper than I planned. Maybe I underestimated how much of a hold Reginald and Angus had on me, but that doesn't mean I want to do what I'm doing. This is for my son. If people have to die to keep him safe, so be it."

"Not just people, bro," Zeke snapped. "Family. That's what this team is. It's what we were supposed to be."

"I tried to protect you, Zeke. I warned you, and that shot at Max? I could have killed him if I'd wanted to. Consider his injury a warning. Next time, I won't miss. I'll be in touch soon, and I'll let you know where the next rendezvous will happen." He disconnected, the sudden silence heavy with tension.

"He needs to be stopped," Julianne muttered, pulling out her phone and punching in the number for head-quarters.

She was calling Dylan.

Ian was certain of that.

Good. He didn't want to talk to anyone.

Not yet.

He needed to collect his thoughts and get himself focused. Two team members had been shot in one night. The situation with the Duprees was escalating. Angus was becoming more desperate. It wasn't just the team and Esme whose lives were at risk. Jake's son and ex-girlfriend might also be in trouble.

He'd let Julianne talk to Dylan, see how Max was and inform the team of the danger. Ian would stick to the plan and follow protocol. It was time to patrol the property.

He called King. The dog came immediately, ready to work or to play. Whichever Ian chose.

For now, they'd just walk, skirting the perimeter of

the property, checking to be sure no one was lurking in the shadows.

Praying that maybe someone was.

Angus would be a good find. Bringing him in would be the culmination of months of hard work and years of planning.

A decade.

That was how long Ian had been waiting to bring the Duprees down.

He didn't want to have to wait any longer, but he would. He'd bide his time as long as it took, and when it was over, when Angus was in jail and the crime syndicate was defunct, he'd finally be able to move forward.

Out from the shadow of anger and hatred.

Into something bright and new.

An image of Esme filled his mind, her soft lips and vivid eyes, her silky hair falling straight to her nape.

Her smile.

A Dupree cut from different cloth. One who deserved all the good life could bring. He wanted to make sure she got it.

But first, he wanted to find her uncle, toss him in jail and throw away the key.

TWELVE

Seven days was a long time to be stuck inside a gaudily decorated swamp shanty. Seven nights was a long time to lie listening to the hushed voices of Ian and his team.

And now she was on night eight.

Doing exactly what she'd done for the past seven.

Counting the opening and closing of the front door, listening to the soft pad of paws on the floor outside her door, to the quiet bark of King as he patrolled the property.

Waiting for dawn to come and something to change.

She turned over in bed, eyeing the tiny cracks in the shades that covered the window. She wanted to pull the cord and open the bright yellow vinyl, to look out into the darkness and watch the moonlight reflected on the water.

She wanted a dozen things that she couldn't have, but mostly she just wanted this to be over.

Sighing, Esme climbed out of bed, padding across the floor on bare feet, wincing as the boards creaked. It was an old place. She'd learned that about it, the rough-hewn floors speaking of a bygone era, the window glass wavy from age.

Not that she was allowed near the windows.

Seven days without sunlight was beginning to get to her.

She could admit that.

If not for Ian, she'd have gone stark raving mad by now. He'd entertained her with stories of his childhood, taught her how to play chess, insisted she teach him how to bake her mother's award-winning pound cake. It was the recipe she used when she was meeting clients for the first time—pound cake and coffee or tea. Making the cake, laughing as she watched Ian measure flour and butter and try his hand at whipping cream had been cathartic.

It felt good to laugh.

It felt good to sit with someone who seemed to want to sit with her. It felt good to play chess and checkers, argue over who'd get the last piece of cake or the last slice of ham.

It wasn't just Ian, though.

She'd become friends with Julianne, offering suggestions on the wedding the FBI agent was planning with Brody Kenner, a man she'd broken up with years ago and had recently reconnected with. She'd run into him while she was searching for Jake Morrow. He'd been sheriff of the small town of Clover, Texas. Now he was training to join the K-9 team.

Julianne had told the story matter-of-factly, but Esme had seen the joy in her eyes and in her face. She'd promised to help her choose colors and decor, find vendors and, maybe, pick a dress.

Ian had heard them talking and gone on a mission, returning hours later with a bagful of wedding magazines.

Zeke had laughed, but he'd sat in the ugly easy chair and given his opinion about the dresses and flowers and food.

Funny. The seven days she'd spent in the ugly house at the edge of the swamp had taught Esme a lot about what friendship was and about what family meant. She could see that was what Zeke, Ian and Julianne were. They were a team, a pack with three leaders, all working together for the good of the group.

She liked that.

But she hated waiting. She hated wondering just how long their little group would stay together.

It wouldn't last forever.

She didn't want it to.

Esme paced back across the room, settling into the rocking chair that Ian had brought for her. She hadn't asked where he'd gotten it or how he'd known that she preferred simple wooden frames and plain blue cushions to anything ornate or fancy. Instead, she'd just thanked him and enjoyed it.

That was the thing about being in the safe house.

Things weren't complicated.

Not unless she thought too much about them.

Then she'd start to wonder and worry and ask herself questions she couldn't answer—like what she was going to do when Angus was finally apprehended and she could move on.

Ian had hinted that they'd move on together.

She liked that idea, but she was trying to enjoy the moment, to take what he was offering now and not question it too much.

Anything could happen while they were waiting for the trial, and this thing they were feeling—this fragile new relationship they were forging—could become old and blasé and boring.

She snorted.

If she were being totally honest with herself, she'd admit she didn't want that to happen. She'd admit that the more time she spent with Ian, the more things she learned about him, the more time she wanted to spend and the more she wanted to know.

She'd never felt that way about Brent.

He'd been a nice guy. She'd liked him. He'd seemed faithful, moral, hardworking—all the things she'd been looking for. He hadn't been the kind of person who'd told stories to make people laugh. He'd told stories to impress, and for a while, he'd impressed her. He'd done all the right things, gone through all the right motions. Flowers. Candy. Expensive dinners.

It had taken a lot of distance and a lot of perspective for her to understand the truth. Brent had been more concerned about what he could get out of the relationship than what he could put in it. Esme had spent the years they were together trying to please him, because she'd thought that was how love was supposed to work. Give and give and give, because that was what the other person expected.

But when she was with Ian, things flowed smoothly. Give and take. Back and forth. Exchanges of ideas and opinions without the need for either of them to be right.

Being with him was as natural as breathing, and she couldn't quite figure out why. Except that he made it easy to be herself. He didn't ask for anything other than the truth. He didn't expect anything more than her company.

The old glider moved beneath her as she pulled her feet up and wrapped her arms around her knees.

The house had gone quiet, the first and second patrol of the night over. If she listened carefully enough, she might hear one of the dogs moving restlessly. Other than that, things would stay quiet for a half hour and then grow busy again.

In a few days, they'd be leaving.

That was what Ian had told her.

He couldn't say where they were going. Just that it would be far away from the Everglades. Esme wasn't sorry about that. She wanted to leave Florida and all the bad memories she had of it. Fortunately, she had some good memories now, though. Memories that she knew would always make her smile.

Esme rested her head on her knees, closing her eyes for just a moment, drifting in the silence and the darkness, the hope of something new and wonderful nudging her into sleep.

She dreamed of Angus. His sharp eyes and hard features. His skinny body and sinewy limbs. She dreamed of his hand in her hair, yanking her backward, tearing at her scalp, his lips pressed close to her ear, screaming words she couldn't understand. In her dream she tried to run, her arms and legs refusing to cooperate. She could see a door. Knew that if she reached it, she would live, but she couldn't move. She was trapped by his grip on her hair and by her fear.

She tried to scream, but nothing but a whimper emerged.

He yanked her backward, slamming her into a wall and shouting into her face. She could see the pockmarks in his skin, the burst spider veins on either side of his nose.

She could see the hatred in his eyes, and, she thought, the evil. Panic-stricken, she clawed at his hand, trying to get him to release his hold, but that only angered him more.

He tossed her away, his hand still in her hair, his fist slamming into the side of her head.

She woke with a start, found herself on the floor, the gliding rocker bumping against her feet.

She'd fallen. That was all. Nothing sinister or scary about that. She sat up, gingerly got to her feet.

Nothing hurt. She was fine, but she felt uneasy, her skin crawling with the kind of fear she hadn't felt since she'd arrived at the safe house.

Somewhere outside, an owl hooted, the sound out of place and alarming.

She crept to the window, breaking the rule that had been drilled into her, pulling back the shades and peering out into the darkness. The owl hooted again, and she was certain she saw a shadow move at the corner of the yard.

Esme needed to get to Ian, let him know that someone was outside. They had to—

Her door opened, and she screamed, the sound shrill and high and filled with terror. She ran at the shadowy form that stood in the doorway, head down, ready to ram right through him if she needed to.

He caught her arm, and she knew the feel of the warm fingers against her skin, the gentleness of the touch.

"Ian," she gasped, and he pulled her up against his chest, whispered in her ear.

"There's someone outside. More than one person, I think. We've got to get out."

"Right." She started to move past, but he stopped her.

"We need to get out, but we need to be smart about it. There's an emergency pack in your closet. Grab that and put on the waders that are sitting beside it."

She'd seen the pack.

She'd even looked through it.

She really hadn't expected to have to use it, though.

Heart thudding in her chest, she ran to the closet, shoving her feet into knee-high waders and slipping into a jacket and then the pack.

Ian was still at the door when she returned, and he took her hand, leading her out into the living room. The lights were off, but she could see Julianne and Zeke standing near the kitchen, their dogs small shadows near their feet.

No one spoke. Esme could only assume they'd had an escape route planned out before they'd ever brought her to the house.

Ian urged her past his colleagues, down the hall that led to the back of the house and the rear deck. There was no way down from there. They'd have to walk around the front to escape.

She was sure Ian knew it, but she wanted to remind him, because she really really didn't want to be trapped on the deck, an easy target to whomever might be stalking them.

She opened her mouth, would have spoken, but one of the dogs growled, the sound sending fear racing up her spine. Esme had heard King growl before, but she'd never heard Thunder or Cheetah make anything but happy noises.

King…

She glanced back. Saw no sign of the dog.

"Where's King?" she whispered, the words barely breaking the silence.

"On the deck."

"He's not barking."

"We don't want our friends to know that we're aware of their presence. He'll only alert if they get closer."

"You said there's more than one?"

"I said I *think* there is," he corrected.

"Does that mean two? Three?"

He touched her cheek, his fingers brushing across her jaw and then her lips, stopping the frantic words.

"It doesn't matter," he said. "However many there are, we'll take care of them."

"Ian—"

"It's going to be okay," he reassured her, pulling her in for a quick hug before slowly opening the back door. Carefully easing outside, he gestured for Esme to follow.

She wanted to move with the same grace and confidence he'd had, but the waders seemed to catch on the old floor, and she nearly fell into the doorjamb.

He caught her, his hands skimming down her arms and resting on her waist.

"Careful," he said, the word more breath than noise.

She nodded but didn't speak again.

They were outside now, the full moon casting long shadows across the backyard. King stood a few feet away, his fur glowing gold in the moon's reflected light.

The canine didn't glance their way as they approached. He didn't move. She didn't think he even blinked. His focus was on the back edge of the property and the deep shadows there. His ears were up, his tail stiff, his posture tense.

Someone was there.

King knew it, and he was ready to act if he received the command.

Ian moved up beside the dog, offering a hand signal that broke King's concentration. The dog trotted to the side of the house, scanned the area and headed back, nudging the back of his handler's calf.

"It's clear. Let's go," Ian whispered, taking her hand and leading her to the area King had just left. He stopped at the deck railing, and she wasn't sure what he thought they were going to do.

Jump?

She sure hoped not. It was twenty feet straight down, and she wasn't all that great at landing. Even if she were, she didn't think she'd manage to do it without breaking something.

Ian slid out of his pack, unzipping the front compartment and taking out a harness. He motioned for King, and the dog loped over, waiting patiently while Ian hooked him in.

"Ready?" he asked Esme, and she nodded even though she still had no idea what they were going to do.

The way she saw things, as long as his plan involved escaping with their lives, she was good with it.

He pulled something else from his pack.

Rope?

No. A ladder.

She watched as he hooked it to the deck railing and let it fall over the side. It made a quiet whoosh as it unfolded, and she had about two seconds to worry that sound had carried to the back of the yard. Then Ian was up, the dog strapped to his chest, as he climbed over the rail and started making his way down the rope ladder.

She was next.

That much was obvious.

She clambered over the railing, trying not to think about the twenty-foot drop as she started down the ladder.

Esme didn't hesitate; she climbed over the railing and scrambled down the ladder like she'd done it a million times before. He helped her down the last two rungs, his hands light against her narrow waist, her pack knocking against his hands.

He'd already released King from his harness and tucked it into the pack. They were ready to head around the front of the property. The dock was there. And the boat. If they were careful, they should be able to escape before their stalkers knew they'd left.

That was good.

What wasn't good was the fact that there were at least two people wandering through the swampy area that surrounded the house. Even if the dogs hadn't been growling and pacing, Ian would have known about the trespassers. He'd been awake and restless when he'd heard the first owl call. By the time he'd heard the second, he'd already gathered the team and put the escape plan into action.

Ian and Esme out the back.

Zeke and Julianne out the front.

They'd gone over the plan dozens of times while they'd waited for Angus to strike.

That was paying off.

He heard the front door open, listened for the quick hard tap of feet on wood.

There!

Julianne and Zeke were heading for the stairs. If things went well, they'd be down in seconds, climbing into the SUV and taking off. Hopefully, leading trouble away.

Ian and Esme would take the boat, rowing out far enough to be out of sight of the house before starting the motor. There was a campsite twenty miles away. Not a long trip, but hazardous at night. Julianne had figured it would take two or three hours to safely navigate. She'd have the SUV there when they arrived.

From there, they'd head straight to headquarters in Montana, and then Esme would be flown out of the country.

She wouldn't like it.

He knew it.

He didn't like it, either. The truth was, he'd wanted to argue for a different location. Somewhere close to headquarters, a place he might be assigned to keep her safe. He'd understood the practicality of Max's decision. He knew that she'd be safer out of the country than in it. The Dupree crime family was a multi-limbed tree, its branches spreading through the United States. With the price on her head, Esme was too vulnerable. No matter where they hid her, there was a good chance she'd be found.

Ian and Max had discussed it. They'd agreed. The only way to keep her safe was to get her out of the country. He cared about her too much to want anything less than her total security. Eventually, she'd return, and when the trial was over, he was going to make certain they were never separated again.

First things first, though.

He tugged her to the edge of the yard, urging her

down into thick grass that was tall enough to cover them both. They crouched there, his hand on her forearm, her head brushing against his shoulder. He wanted to tell her everything would be okay, wanted to remind her that he'd make sure of it. Instead, he pulled her closer, did what he would have done days ago if there hadn't always been someone around; he pressed a kiss to her forehead, her cheek, her lips. Soft. Easy. Tender, because that was how it felt to be around her.

The SUV's engine roared. Tires squealed.

He backed away, his heart thundering, his pulse racing. Not with fear. With longing for all the things he hadn't been looking for but had found in Esme. He could see her through the darkness, her face pale, her eyes wide.

"What was that?" she whispered, her fingers touching her lips.

"A promise."

"Of what?"

"Tomorrow and the next day and the next," he said, his lips brushing her ear as he spoke.

Somewhere in the distance, an owl called, the sound chilling Ian's blood.

That was the signal he'd been waiting for. The one that told him the enemy was on the move.

Beside him, King growled, a long low warning that Ian wasn't going to ignore.

The SUV pulled out of the carport, headlights flashing on the ground a few feet away. There. Gone. Julianne and Zeke were doing their part.

It was time to do his.

"Let's go," he whispered, pulling Esme through the

thick grass and boggy water, the roaring engine masking the sound of their retreat.

They made it to the dock easily. He climbed onto it, pulling Esme up beside him, King growling and barking, trying to tell him something that took just a few seconds too long for Ian to figure out.

By the time he did, it was too late.

Angus was there, rising like a wraith from the boat, a gun in his hand.

Ian reached for his firearm.

"Stop," Angus said calmly. "I've got nothing against you, Ian. It's Esme I have a problem with."

"I've got a problem with you, too," Esme retorted. "So I guess the feeling is mutual."

"Shut up," Angus snapped. "Get in the boat."

"Or what? You'll kill me?" She was baiting him, trying to keep his attention. Maybe so that Ian could act. Or maybe so that she could.

He felt her shift, thought she might be planning to dive off the dock and into the swamp. She probably figured she'd have a better chance there than she would with her uncle.

Or, maybe, she thought she'd draw Angus's gunfire away from Ian, give him a chance to pull his gun and end the fight.

Ian wasn't going to let her do it.

He gave the command, and King took off, sailing through the air, knocking into Angus with so much force the other man went down, the gun going off as he landed.

One shot, but it was followed by another. This one coming from somewhere near the house. King was snarling, teeth around Angus's wrist, shaking it so hard the gun flew out of his hand and landed somewhere beside the dock.

Ian didn't have time to go after it.

A bullet whizzed by his ear, coming so close he thought he could feel the heat of it. He dived for cover, taking Esme with him, rolling off the dock as more bullets flew.

They landed in soft wet earth, and he covered her with his body, holding her in place when she tried to stand.

Suddenly, King was beside them. He'd disarmed Angus, and he was back, ready to do more.

Ian raised a hand, giving the command to apprehend, and King took off again, racing toward the house and whoever was firing the weapon.

Ian heard the growls and snarls of the fight, heard a man cry out in agony. There were no high-pitched yips from King. Which meant he wasn't being hurt, and that he'd taken the gunman by surprise.

Another human yowl, and the night went silent.

No noise but the soft lap of water against the shore.

"Is it over?" Esme mumbled against his chest. "Because you're suffocating me."

"Sorry." He backed off, caught the unmistakable coppery scent of blood, saw black rivulets of it running down Esme's arm.

"You've been hit," he growled, pulling off his jacket and pressing it against the wound.

She pushed his hand away.

"I'm fine. Go help King."

"King can take care of himself." He knew that for a fact, was certain the dog was already on his way back. He glanced around, searching the shadows for Angus. The guy had disappeared, but that didn't mean he was gone.

"Really." She stood and took a step away. "I'm okay. Call your dog back, and let's get in the boat and get out of here."

"I'm afraid that isn't going to happen." Angus moved out of the shadows of an old mangrove tree, a gun drawn and pointed, hand bloody from his fight with King. He'd obviously been carrying a second weapon. Something Ian would have checked for if he'd had the opportunity.

Ian reached for his Glock, freezing when Angus pointed the revolver at Esme's head.

"Don't," he said conversationally. "Not unless you'd like to see her die."

He let his hand fall away, let Angus think he had the upper hand.

"That's better," the older man said, grabbing the back of Esme's jacket and yanking her toward him. He slammed the barrel of the gun into her temple, and she winced, her reaction making Ian want to pull his Glock and take a chance that he could fire before Angus.

It was too big a risk, though. If he timed it wrong, she'd be dead.

"Now, take out the gun and toss it in the water. Slowly. Try anything funny, and Esme's brains will be splattered all over the swamp."

"Ian, don't do it. He's going to kill me anyway," Esme pleaded.

"It'll be okay," he said, looking into her eyes, willing her to calm down, to trust him. "I promise."

"Right. And promises mean so much," Angus sneered. "Toss the gun. Now."

Ian pulled it from the holster, looking straight into Esme's panicked eyes as he did exactly what he had been told.

THIRTEEN

They were going to die.

Esme wasn't certain of much, but she was sure of that.

Not only had Ian tossed his gun into the swamp, but he'd sent King off to chase down another gunman. Which would have been fine if Uncle Angus hadn't been armed with a second weapon.

The first one, the one King had shaken from his hand, had looked deadly enough. This one looked even worse.

Maybe because the barrel was pressed against her head.

"Happy?" Ian asked. The question was obviously meant for Angus, but he was still looking into her eyes.

He didn't look panicked.

He didn't look scared. She'd have found that comforting if she didn't know just how deadly the situation was.

"Very," Angus crowed. "This is what I like to see! Absolute obedience. Keep it up, *Fed*-boy, and you might just survive."

"I'm more concerned about Esme. How about we agree that she won't testify if you let her go?"

"Sorry. That's not going to happen. First, because she's caused me a lot of trouble, and I'm ready to make her pay for that. Second, because I don't trust you, her or the United States government."

"We could offer something else in exchange for her life."

"Like what?" The gun dropped away, just a fraction of an inch, but it was enough to give Esme a little hope and a little wiggle room. If it dropped any farther, she'd elbow him in the stomach and make a run for it.

As if he sensed her thoughts, Ian met her eyes again, offering a subtle shake of his head.

A warning, she thought.

A week ago, she would have ignored it and gone ahead with her plan. Now she knew Ian. She knew how his mind worked, how he thought, the way he worked. He didn't believe in taking chances. He always had a plan A, a plan B and a plan C. He'd told her that one night while they were playing checkers.

Tonight's plan A hadn't worked out.

Maybe plan B would be better.

And maybe she'd be smart to wait a little longer, see what Ian had up his sleeve.

"Here's what I'm thinking," Ian said, shuffling forward a couple of steps.

"What *I'm* thinking," Angus barked, "is that you need to stay where you are."

"Sorry. I was thinking about other things. Like you. On a plane, heading for a tropical paradise."

"That sounds more like your friend Jake's cup of tea," Angus said, tugging Esme backward, dragging her into ankle-deep water.

"Jake's smart. He knows that the best way to stay out of jail is to get out of the country."

"He's smart, all right," Angus agreed. "I showed him a few pictures of this place, told him how many people were working protection, and he was able to tell me exactly how you'd react if you were under attack. He knew you'd send your friends off in the SUV. He knew you'd try to escape in the boat. He even knew that you'd only keep one dog back at the house."

"Like I said," Ian replied, no heat in his voice, no emotion. He was getting ready to move, Esme could sense it. She could feel the tension in him, the corded muscles and tamped-down energy. All of it was ready to explode. "Jake is smart. You'd be wise to take a page from his book."

"Meaning?"

"Agree to let us fly you out of the country. Stay away for good, and you won't have to worry about the police or the feds."

"I'm not much for tropical climates," Angus said, his beady eyes shifting from Ian to a point just beyond his shoulder. "That you, Eddie?" he called.

There was no reply, and he took another step back, dragging Esme with him.

She wasn't sure what he'd seen. She didn't care.

She just didn't want to have to take another step deeper into the water, because she had the horrible feeling she knew what he planned. One gunshot, and her body would fall, the loud splash attracting predators for miles around.

She'd probably be dead before they reached her.

The thought wasn't comforting.

"Who's Eddie?" Ian asked.

"One of the guys I hired to help out. Four people to help me take you down and get my niece. That's what Jake said."

"Did he also say that I don't like to be fooled?" Ian asked. "And that I always make sure that I'm well armed?"

He moved so quickly, Esme almost didn't see it happen.

First he was still, then he was beside her, one arm sweeping in a downward arc, a glittering knife heading straight for Angus's hand.

Angus shrieked, jerking away, but maintaining his grip on the gun.

"Move!" Ian shouted, giving Esme a gentle shove toward shore.

She stumbled, landing on her knees, blood sleeping down her arm and dripping into the dark water.

Get up! her mind shrieked. *Run!*

She was finally up, stumbling through the water, screaming for King, hoping the dog would come running.

Praying he would.

Suddenly, he was there, flying across the yard, splashing into the water. He moved past, aiming for the struggling men, launching himself into the air and into the fray.

Angus cursed, stumbling from the pack, the gun still in his hand, his arms bloody and oozing.

He lifted the weapon, and King charged again.

"No!" Esme screamed, but it was too late.

The gun report was deafening, the sound drowning out everything else. She watched in horror, expecting King to fall away, but he was still moving, landing against Angus, pushing him over.

Or...

Maybe Angus was just falling, the gun splashing into the swamp as the sound of the gunshot faded away.

"I'd feel bad, but he deserved it," a woman said, her voice so close to Esme's ear, she screamed, whirling around and looking straight into her sister's gorgeous face.

Violetta Dupree had saved King's life.

No matter how hard he tried, Ian couldn't wrap his mind around that. He took another sip of the hot coffee Julianne had offered him, eyeing Esme's sister over the top of the paper cup.

She perched on the edge of a vinyl-covered chair in the waiting room of the ER.

She looked...

Tired.

Undone.

Her brown hair fell in messy waves around her pale face. Her mascara was smeared underneath her eyes. She'd been wearing red lipstick at some point, and lines of it feathered out from her lips. She was a beautiful woman. There was no doubt about that, but she looked like she'd aged ten years since he'd last seen her, and that had been only a couple of months ago.

"I don't understand what's taking so long," she complained, biting at a hangnail on the edge of her thumb. "You said the gunshot wound didn't look that bad."

"It didn't."

"Then why haven't they come to let us know how Esme is doing?"

"It takes time to clean a wound," Julianne offered, and Violetta huffed.

"It would be nice if it would take a little less time. I have things to do." She flicked a speck of mud off her dark jeans and frowned.

"What kind of things?" Ian asked, trying to see a little of Esme in her face.

"Nothing that concerns you or your people. A friend is having a birthday party this weekend, and I need to be home for it."

"So you just took a little jaunt from Chicago to Florida to kill your uncle, and now you're going back home to hobnob with your rich friends?" Zeke's assessment was harsh, and Violetta's eyes widened.

"I did not come out here to kill Angus. I came to save my sister."

"And you knew she was in trouble because…?" Juli-anne tapped her fingers on her thighs and eyed Violetta with a mixture of curiosity and suspicion.

It was the same look Ian was probably giving her.

Violetta didn't answer questions. At least, not any questions he'd ever asked. Now she seemed determined to tell them everything she knew.

As long as it was on her time frame.

"It was pretty obvious that our uncle wanted Esme dead, and that he wasn't going to stop going after her until he achieved his goal."

"You didn't seem all that concerned about her well-being when we tried to get you to tell us what you knew about your uncle," Ian pointed out, and she shrugged, flipping a strand of hair over her shoulder.

"Of course I was concerned. Esme means the world to me."

"Do I?" Esme's voice carried through the small wait-ing area, and Ian turned, saw her standing in the doorway. Her arm was in a sling, her hair was slicked to her scalp, her face was pale and streaked with mud.

And she was absolutely the most beautiful woman he'd ever seen. King must have thought the same. He barreled toward her, stopping at her feet and looking up at her adoringly.

"Hello, handsome," Esme said, swaying a little as she leaned down to pet the dog.

Ian cupped the elbow of her good arm, supporting her weight as she straightened.

"Thanks," she said, smiling into his eyes.

And, right then, he knew. Beyond a shadow of a doubt. Knew more than he knew almost anything else, that he'd be in Esme's life for as long as she wanted him there.

"It's not hard to give someone a hand when they need it," he said, helping her to the seat next to her sister.

"I meant for everything else," she replied, looking into his eyes and offering a soft sweet smile. "You've given up a lot to keep me safe, and I appreciate that more than I can say."

"You won't be safe until after you testify. You do know that, don't you?" Violetta lifted Esme's hand and squeezed it gently. "There are still plenty of people who would like Reginald to go free."

"I don't suppose you want to name any of them?" Julianne asked, and Violetta stiffened.

"Of course she doesn't," Zeke cut in. "She's willing to help her sister, but only if it doesn't interfere with her life."

"You have no idea what you're talking about." Violetta stood, her body nearly shaking with fury. "I have done nothing but help you people. I've kept my silence so that I could keep track of Jake Morrow. I knew he'd keep in touch with Angus, and I was right."

"You know where Jake is?" Zeke asked, and Violetta shook her head.

"I've heard he's going after his ex-girlfriend and his son. He won't leave the country without them."

"Who did you hear that from?" Esme prodded, leaning back in the seat and stifling a yawn. She was trying to cover up how bone-tired she was, but Ian noticed.

"Angus. I kept on his good side so that I could protect you. That was my only reason, my sole motivation. I hope you believe that, Esme."

"So you've been playing up to your uncle and getting information from him?" Julianne had taken a small notepad from her pocket and was jotting something in it. "Is that what you're saying?"

"That is exactly what I'm saying. I've made my mistakes. I'll admit that. I like nice things. Expensive things. I was happy to let my brother and uncle get them for me." Her gaze shifted to her sister, and she frowned. "But I love you more than any of that, Esme. I would have cooperated with the FBI immediately if I hadn't been afraid it would cost you your life."

"Sounds to me like you're trying to separate yourself from your brother's crimes," Zeke said, and Violetta scowled.

"You don't know a thing about me. None of you do. If I'd wanted to separate myself from my brother's crimes, I wouldn't be here. I'd have stopped Angus, and I'd have gone straight back to Chicago without letting any of you know I'd been here. It wasn't like you weren't distracted enough for me to escape. I stayed because I accomplished my goal. Everything I've done these past months has been to protect my sister."

"If that's the case, you shouldn't be hesitating to give us information about the way the organization runs," Ian accused.

"I'm afraid, okay?" Violetta nearly shouted. "Not all of us are like Esme—brave enough to risk our lives. I'm not. I never have been. Except when it comes to her. I'd do anything to keep her safe. Even play to my uncle's good side, pretend to be part of his team and convince him to confide in me." She hissed out a breath. "He told me all about Jake Morrow. He told me that he'd threatened Jake's son's and ex-girlfriend's lives. It made me physically ill. Who would hurt a child?"

"Your uncle," Ian said, gentling his voice, because he believed her, and he was starting to feel sympathy for the mess she'd found herself in.

"I know," she said just as gently, her gaze on her sister. "I'm so sorry this happened, Esme. If I could go back and change things, make different decisions, be a better person, I would. I promise you that."

"You can make different decisions," Julianne said, and there didn't seem to be a hint of sympathy in her voice. "As long as Jake Morrow is free, your sister may not be safe. Angus was a terrible person, but Reginald calls the shots. He may be trying to contact Jake, get him to follow through on the effort to silence Esme before the trial. We need to bring him in, and we need to do it quickly if you really want to keep your sister from harm."

Violetta frowned. "Some of the information I got was vague, but I'll tell you what I know. Angus told me Jake was going back home to find his ex-girlfriend and his baby. She despises what he's become and wants nothing to do with him, but he's not going to leave the country until he has his son."

The words jolted through Ian, and he fished his phone out of his pocket, scrolled through the texts until he found the one sent by Anonymous: Word is that Mommy, Daddy and child have gone home.

"You're Anonymous," he said, and she blushed.

"Yes. Like I said, I was trying to pass on as much information as I could without making things too easy to figure out."

"Easy would have been nice," Zeke grumbled.

"Easy would have gotten me killed," she responded through clenched teeth, dropping into the seat beside Esme. "I was the only one who knew about Jake Morrow. If I'd given you too much information and you'd passed it on to someone owned by Angus..." She shuddered.

"Tell us about Jake going home," Ian demanded, turning the subject back to the thing he was most interested in.

He didn't really care what Violetta's motivation had been. It didn't matter to him if it had been greed or fear that had caused her to get close to her uncle. What he cared about was the fact that she had information that could prove to be very useful to the team.

"He's in Montana. At least, that's where I think he is. Angus thought it was hilarious that he was going to be so close to your headquarters. He liked to say you were all farsighted, unable to see what was right in front of your faces."

"What else did he like to say?" Zeke asked, his irritation and anger obvious.

"That he was smarter than all of you put together. That he always came out on top, and the rest of us were flies buzzing around on the trash heap of his leftovers." She squeezed the bridge of her nose and shook her head. "He really was a horrible man."

"Maybe you should have gone to the police and told them that a long time ago." Zeke stalked out of the room, Cheetah bounding along beside him.

"I already said that I'd change things if I could. What more do you people want from me?" Violetta began, her frustration and irritation obvious.

Ian had the feeling that she was just gearing up, that she had a whole lot more she wanted to say about the way they were treating her.

Esme held up her hand, stopping her sister's diatribe.

"Do we have to do this right now?" she asked wearily.

"Of course we do," Violetta retorted. "I didn't come all this way to be treated like a criminal."

"Just stop, Violetta," Esme said. "It's been a long day. Actually, it's been a long six months. I'm tired, and I just want to go home. Except—" Her voice broke, and a tear rolled down her cheek. "I can't, because I have to keep drifting from place to place until the trial. You get to go back to the fancy penthouse Reginald helped you buy. Until his trial is over and he's been sentenced, there's no place that I'll ever feel safe. No place to throw anchor and wait until the storm blows over. I just have to keep riding it out until the bitter end."

"Oh. Honey! I'm sorry. I wasn't thinking about what you've been through." Violetta pulled tissue from her handbag and tried to give them to Esme.

Esme nudged them away.

"Esme," Violetta tried again. "Don't cry. None of these people are worth your tears."

"Yes. They are. And so are you. So, please, let's not do this right now." She swiped at the errant tear, her hand shaking.

Julianne met Ian's eyes. "You want me to handle the interrogation?"

"Yes. And update Max on the case. He'll be interested in hearing the information about Jake."

She nodded, touching Violetta's shoulder and somehow convincing her to walk out of the room.

Turning back to Esme, he saw that her eyes were closed. She had her head resting against the wall and her hands fisted in her lap, and when another tear slipped down her cheek, he couldn't hold back.

He lifted her good hand, unfurled her fingers and pressed a kiss to her palm.

"What's that for?" she murmured, not opening her eyes.

"Something to anchor you until you find your way home," he said, and she smiled, but the tears kept falling, and he finally tugged her into his lap, pressed her head to his chest and just let her cry.

FOURTEEN

She hated crying.

Hated it, but she couldn't seem to stop. The tears kept rolling down her face, soaking into Ian's shirt.

Ian!

She was cradled in his arms.

Crying all over him.

She pushed away, her left arm shrieking in protest.

Because she'd been shot.

By her uncle.

Her own flesh and blood, but he'd wanted her dead. In the end, he'd died because of that.

"Slow down," Ian said as she scrambled away from him.

"Your shirt is soaked," she pointed out.

"And?"

"I'd die of embarrassment. If that were actually a thing."

"What's to be embarrassed about?" He snagged her hand, holding her in place when she would have backed farther away.

"Look at me!" She gestured to her mud-encrusted pants, her hair, her tear-soaked face. "I'm a mess!"

"A beautiful mess," he responded gruffly, and her heart did a funny little dance. One that spoke of happiness and contentment and better things to come.

And suddenly the tears weren't sliding down her cheeks anymore. Suddenly, she was smiling. "Only you would say something like that," she said.

"And I'd only say it to you. How's the arm?"

"Sore, but I'll live."

"And the heart?"

"The same." Her voice broke, and the stupid tears started again.

"They'll both get better. Just give it a little time." He tugged her into his arms, his lips brushing hers. Once. Then again. Her hand slid up his arm, her fingers slid through his hair.

She could have stood there with him forever, tasting the sweetness of his lips, feeling the warmth of his hand resting on her back.

Someone cleared his throat, and she jerked back, nearly tripping over King.

"Sorry," she said to the dog, and his tail thumped.

"I'm probably the one who should be apologizing. I didn't mean to interrupt," a man said, and she turned, watching as he walked into the room. Tall and blond with a scar that slashed down the side of his cheek, he had the bluest eyes she'd ever seen.

"Max," Ian said. If he were embarrassed at having been caught kissing her, he didn't show it. "What are you doing here?"

"I decided to come help with the transport. The more people protecting Ms. Dupree, the better. I took the redeye last night. If I'd known how much trouble you were going to be in, I'd have tried to get to Florida sooner."

He smiled, offering Esme his hand. "I'm Max West. Team captain and shameless romantic."

"Really?"

"No, but I thought it might make things less awkward."

"I really don't think anything can do that."

"Well, then how about we focus on the business at hand? Has Ian explained what our next step is?"

"There hasn't been a whole lot of time," Ian said, and Max nodded.

"Right. So here's how it's going to be, Esme. We're going to take you to our headquarters in Montana. You'll be there until our next safe house is ready."

"Is it going to be in a swamp?" she asked, too tired to argue with the plan.

"No." He laughed. "It's going to be really nice. Not in the States, though. We've arranged for you to have round-the-clock security in another country. We've already collected your passport. If there's anything else you think you'll need, let us know and we'll make sure you have it."

Yeah.

There was.

She'd need Ian, but she didn't think that was what Max was expecting to hear.

"Some air would be nice. If that's okay," she said, offering a poor facsimile of a smile.

She didn't think either of the men bought it, but neither tried to stop her. With Angus dead, she was safe. At least until Reginald could figure out a way to hire killers from prison.

Throat thick with emotion, she reached the exit and walked out into early-morning light. The sun was just peeking above the horizon, the ground dusted gold with it. King appeared at her side, his sturdy body pressing against her leg, warm and heavy and comforting.

"It's going to be okay," she murmured.

"Yes, it is," Ian said, and she wasn't surprised that he was there, wasn't shocked when he turned her so that they were facing each other.

"I don't want to leave the country," she said. Simple. Straightforward. To the point.

"I'm sorry," he responded, and she knew his hands were tied, that the decision wasn't his. "But your sister will be fine. She's very good at taking care of herself."

"That's not what I'm worried about."

"Then what?" he asked. "Your business? Your friends?" He touched her chin, offered a smile that should have made her heart sing. It just made her think of what she'd almost had, and what she was about to lose.

"You," she finally admitted, and he shook his head, tugged her into his arms, pressed her head to his chest.

"Why would you think I'd let you?"

"Because your work is here, and I'm going to be somewhere else."

"My work is with you. Keeping you safe is my assignment until after the trial. King and I have both been cleared to travel with you. I sent Max a text while you were getting your arm cleaned up. He was quick to agree to the plan."

"What if the trial takes years to happen?"

"I don't care if it takes a lifetime, Esme. As long as we're together."

"Are you sure?"

"Absolutely. Now, how about we go back inside and get started on our new adventure?" He took her hand, leading her back to the door. King loped beside him, his ears up, his nose to the air.

He stopped short, whining softly.

"What is it, King?" Ian asked, touching the dog's broad head.

"Is someone out here with us?"

"He'd be barking, but there's definitely something worrying him."

King whined again.

"Find it," Ian said, and the dog took off, racing around the side of the building, nose still to the air, ears alert.

They moved through an alley and then into a back lot.

That was when Esme heard it. Above the distant sound of morning traffic, above the pounding of her heart, the soft whimpering cry of an animal in distress.

"What in the world?" she asked, but Ian was striding across the back lot, following King to a Dumpster that butted against a brick wall.

"Whatever it is," he said, lifting the lid and peering inside, "it's in here."

"Maybe we should call animal control," she suggested as King stood on two legs and looked inside the bin.

She looked, too, because she had to.

The crying was pitiful, and whatever was making the sound needed help.

"I think we can handle this," Ian said, reaching for a box that was shoved up against the back of the metal container. Someone had taped it closed, and the thing inside bumped against the top.

"What if it's a rat?" She cringed as he pulled a utility tool from his pocket and carefully sliced through the tape.

"King wouldn't be going crazy over a rodent. I think it's a—"

He didn't get a chance to finish.

The lid popped open, and a dark-faced thing appeared.

No. Not a thing.

A puppy. Scrawny. All legs, boxy head and little potbelly, he tried to jump out of the box but ended up falling back in.

King nudged the puppy with his nose, offering a tentative lick.

"Good boy, King," Ian said. "Good find."

He lifted the puppy from what would have been its coffin, checked its gums, felt its ribs.

"He's skinny and dehydrated, but it's nothing a little food and water can't fix."

"Should we take him to the shelter?" she asked, touching the puppy's velvety nose and losing a little piece of her heart when he licked her hand.

"It would probably be the practical thing to do, but there's a lot more to life than practicality. I'm supposed to be looking for a puppy to bring back to our training facility. Kind of a reminder that we're part of a family of sorts, one that always sticks together."

There was a note of sadness in his voice, and she knew he must be thinking about Jake Morrow.

"You are a real family," she told him, because it was the only thing she could offer. "I felt that when we were in the safe house. Just because one member decided to go his own way, doesn't mean the remainder can't stay strong."

"I know, but thanks for the reminder. Some days I

need it more than others," he confided, smiling in the way that always made her heart leap.

"So…what now?"

"Now we'll take this guy inside and introduce him to his new family," he said, holding the puppy in the crook of his arm. "We'll get him checked out by a vet, and we'll take him to puppy training school."

"He'll be an A student. Of course," she joked, feeling lighter than she had in weeks, happier than she'd been in months.

All the hard times, all the difficulties, had led her to this point, and for the first time since she'd witnessed her brother's crime, she was thankful for them.

"Of course," Ian agreed. "No kid of ours could ever be anything less."

"Kid of ours?" she asked.

"A figure of speech," he responded. "And maybe a conversation to revisit at another time."

"I think I'd like that."

"That's what I was hoping you'd say." He grinned, and she couldn't help returning his smile.

"I guess we'll have plenty of time to discuss it and everything else while we're waiting for Reginald's trial," she said.

"And plenty of time after the trial is over," he replied, tugging her close, offering a kiss that promised everything she'd ever hoped for and more.

When he backed away, they were both breathless, and they were both smiling. She noticed that. Just like she noticed the quiet hum of morning traffic, the soft trill of a songbird on a branch nearby. The sun glinting in Ian's dark hair, the puppy sleeping in the crook of his arm, King grinning at his feet.

It all looked fresh and bright and beautiful.

"What was that for?" she asked, and he took her hand.

"You," he said, "and our new beginning."

She laughed. "New beginnings are wonderful things. Especially when we get to start them with people we care about."

"You're right," he agreed. "So how about we get started on ours?"

"That," she replied, levering up on her toes and offering him one more sweet kiss, "sounds like a wonderful idea."

He called to King, and they walked back to the hospital. All of them together. And it was enough to fill all the empty spots in her heart. It was enough to sustain her through whatever the future might bring.

She hadn't wanted the trouble she'd found herself in, but she couldn't regret where it had led her. Where God had led her. Not just to a new beginning, but to the only place where she'd ever truly felt at home.

EPILOGUE

Ian didn't do nervous. He didn't know what it meant to be anxious. He'd spent years working in law enforcement and facing down thugs, druggies and murderers.

He didn't sweat.

He didn't panic.

He didn't lose his cool.

He was an FBI agent, trained to handle whatever crisis came his way.

So why was he sweating now? Beads of perspiration dotting his brow?

Why were his hands shaking as he tried to knot his tie. *For the tenth time.*

Why was his throat dry? His heart pounding? His pulse racing?

"Need some help with that, Ian?" Max said, a hint of amusement in his voice as he eyed Ian's unknotted tie.

He'd dressed up for the occasion—button-up shirt, dark slacks and a small rose that someone had tucked in his pocket. Probably Katarina. Ian wasn't the only one who'd found love while the team was looking for Jake. Max had found it, too. So had several other team members.

"I've got it," he said, smoothing the tie, and patting his jacket pocket. The ring was there. No box, because he hadn't wanted Esme to notice it. They'd come to headquarters to sign last-minute paperwork before they boarded the plane that would take them to a top secret location.

Even Ian wasn't sure exactly where they'd be.

As long as he was with Esme, he really didn't care.

"Is she here yet?" he asked. He'd spent most of the past few weeks at the safe house, but last night he'd had to pack his bags and get ready for the flight. He'd left Esme with three team members, but he'd still been worried.

Now he was just anxious to see her again.

Ten hours wasn't long, but it felt like a lifetime when you were away from the person you loved, the person you wanted to spend a lifetime with.

"Just arrived. I asked Julianne to keep her in the lobby for another minute." He glanced at his watch. "I've sent your bags ahead, and they're already being loaded onto the plane."

"Is that a hint that I should get this show on the road?"

"Not at all. Take your time. It's a private jet. It's not like it's going to leave without you."

"Then again," Dylan O'Leary said, glancing up from a computer he'd been working on, "things have been calm for a couple of weeks. That usually means trouble is brewing. You might want to get out of town before it arrives."

"Don't rush a man who's about to take one of the biggest steps of his life," Zeke responded, crossing the room and taking one of the cookies that team member Harper Prentiss had brought for the occasion.

"Hands off," she said, slapping his hand away. "Those are for after he pops the question."

She turned to Ian, gave him a quick once-over.

"You could have tried a little harder," she announced, straightening his tie.

"Meaning?"

"A tux? A bowtie? A huge bouquet of her favorite flowers?"

"I've been a little busy," he muttered. It was the truth. He'd spent the past three weeks working at the safe house and helping the team as they tried to locate Jake Morrow. So far, they'd come up empty. If Violetta had been right, if he was in Montana, they hadn't been able to find him.

Yet.

Zeke was still looking.

Or he would be once his doctor cleared him to go back to work. The little flesh wound he'd gotten in the shoot-out had been a bigger deal than he'd thought, and he wasn't happy about it.

As far as Ian could tell, he wasn't happy about a lot of things. Ian couldn't blame him. This had been a tough season for the entire team, but looking around the small conference room, he couldn't help thinking how blessed they all were.

They'd cut the Dupree crime family off at the roots.

With Angus dead and Reginald in prison, the organization was dying, crushed by its inability to run itself. He'd heard of at least a dozen arrests in cities all over the country.

And that was the kind of news he would never ever

get tired of listening to. For a long time, he'd thought that was all he wanted, that seeing the crime family destroyed was all he'd needed to make his life complete.

Every time he looked at Esme, every time their eyes met or their hands touched or he heard her soft laughter, he realized just how wrong he'd been.

That still didn't make this any less nerve-racking!

He ran his hand over his hair, tugged at his tie.

"Ian, really!" Harper brushed his hands away from the tie. "Stop fidgeting. You're making a mess of this."

She straightened the tie again.

"Leave the poor guy alone," Dylan said, glancing down at his phone and frowning.

"Trouble?" Max asked.

"About as big a trouble as a guy like me can get into," he responded.

"Meaning?" Ian prodded. He'd much rather focus on someone else's troubles than his out-of-control nerves.

"I'm going to have to go to a…" Dylan sighed. "To a dress shop to pick up Zara's wedding gown. She says they're in hiding and formulating a plan, but the dress is in, and she needs me to get it."

"That's it?"

"Yes."

"That doesn't sound so bad," Ian said.

"Have you ever been to one of those places?"

"No. Have you?"

"Of course not, and I wasn't planning to." He sighed, and Ian would have said something else, maybe offered a solution to the problem, but the door opened and Julianne walked in, Esme right behind her.

His breath caught, and he was sure his heart stopped. She was that beautiful, short red hair framing her face, her sundress skimming slim muscular legs. She'd put a sweater on over the dress, probably hoping to keep warm on the plane. The white knit seemed to highlight the vibrancy of her hair and her eyes.

"You're beautiful," he said.

"So are you," she replied, and he was pretty certain someone laughed. He didn't care. Didn't look to see who it was.

She was all that mattered.

King had walked over, was leaning against Esme's leg, offering a K-9 hug that made her smile.

Ian would normally smile, too, maybe comment on how much King loved her, how quickly he'd accepted her as part of the pack.

He didn't do either, he was too busy studying her face, memorizing the way she looked, so that he could tell their children exactly how gorgeous she'd been the day he'd proposed.

"What's wrong, Ian?" she said, probably sensing his nervous energy.

"I've been thinking," he said. "That I don't want to go into witness protection as your bodyguard. I wan—"

"I understand, Ian." She cut him off before he could finish, obviously assuming something that had never occurred to him.

"I don't think you do," he responded, taking her hand and pulling her closer, mentally kicking himself for making her think for even a moment that he'd walk away. "I don't want to go into witness protection as your bodyguard, because I'm hoping to change my job title before we get on the plane."

"To what?" She looked confused and relieved, her smile returning.

"Fiancé?" he suggested, pulling the ring from his pocket. He had purchased it at an antiques store, the teardrop-shaped emerald surrounded by small mine-cut diamonds, the gold band carved with dozens of infinity symbols.

Her eyes widened when she saw it, and she met his gaze.

"Ian," she breathed, and he didn't know what she meant to say. He only knew what he had to tell her.

The words spilled out. Not practiced or rehearsed. Not the canned little speech that a few of his buddies had suggested. Esme deserved so much more than that.

"I didn't realize what I was missing until I found you, Esme. You are everything I didn't know I was looking for, everything I didn't know I needed. When I'm with you, I'm home. When I'm not, all I can think about is finding my way back. I'd give all I have to spend the rest of my life with you. Will you marry me?"

"Yes," she said, the word choking out as she reached for him, pulled him in for a hug that spoke all the words she hadn't said.

He could hear them in the quiet hitch of her breath, the soft whisper of her hair against his jacket as she laid her head against his chest.

He could have stood with her forever, let that one perfect moment continue, but King nudged his hand, and he realized he was still holding the ring.

He looked down into Esme's face, smiling into her eyes as he slipped the ring on her finger.

"I love you," he said.

"I love you, too," she responded, a single tear sliding down her cheek.

"Then why are you crying?"

"Because this is the most beautiful moment I have ever lived, and I'm so glad I'm living it with you." She offered a watery smile, and he wiped the tear away, kissing her gently, letting the sound of his friends' warm congratulations fill his heart as he took her hand, signaled for King and walked out of the room and into their future together.

* * * * *

If you enjoyed BODYGUARD, look for the next book in the CLASSIFIED K-9 UNIT *series,* TRACKER *by Lenora Worth.*

And don't miss a book in the series:

GUARDIAN *by Terri Reed*
SHERIFF *by Laura Scott*
SPECIAL AGENT *by Valerie Hansen*
BOUNTY HUNTER *by Lynette Eason*
BODYGUARD *by Shirlee McCoy*
TRACKER *by Lenora Worth*
CLASSIFIED K-9 UNIT CHRISTMAS *by Terri Reed and Lenora Worth*

Available now from Love Inspired Suspense!

Find more great reads at www.LoveInspired.com

Dear Reader,

When I first began writing for Love Inspired, my children were young. I worked late at night because it was the only time when I didn't have a toddler in my lap or "Mom!" ringing in my ears. I was so excited to be an author and to share my stories with others. I sat down to write my first reader letter, and I froze. I had no idea what to say! All these years later, that still happens.

Nevertheless, I've found that my words reach the people they are intended for. Perhaps this letter is yours. Perhaps these words are meant for your heart. Because you matter. You do. You are not just a tiny dot on a small planet floating in the darkness of a vast universe. You are a bright light in the life of the people who love you. You are infinitely valuable to your creator, immensely loved by a God who sees your faults and still calls you His. Wherever your road has taken you, I hope that you find comfort in knowing He is there. And if you have lost your way, I pray He leads you safely home.

As always, I would love to hear from you! You can reach me at shirlee@shirleemccoy.com or find me on Facebook, Twitter or Instagram.

Blessings,

Shirlee McCoy

Get 2 Free Books,
Plus 2 Free Gifts—
just for trying the
Reader Service!

Reward the book lover in you!

Earn points from all your Harlequin book purchases from wherever you shop.

Turn your points into *FREE BOOKS* of your choice
OR
EXCLUSIVE GIFTS from your favorite authors or series.

Join for FREE today at
www.HarlequinMyRewards.com.

Harlequin My Rewards is a free program (no fees) without any commitments or obligations.

MYR17